THE CHALET SCHOOL AND
RICHENDA

Gr. 9

This Armada book belongs to:

Shona Eakins
29 Scarlett ave
London, Ontario
N6G 123

THE
CHALET SCHOOL
AND RICHENDA

ELINOR M. BRENT-DYER

First published in the U.K. in 1958 by
W. & R. Chambers Ltd., London and Edinburgh.
This edition was first published in Armada in 1982 by
Fontana Paperbacks, 14 St. James's Place,
London SW1A 1PS.

Made and printed in Great Britain by
William Collins Sons & Co. Ltd, Glasgow

To

MY DEAREST CISSIE
(A.F.J. Warren-Swettenham)

with much love from
ELINOR

CONTENTS

Chapter I

A Khang-he Vase

"Richenda!"

There was no reply, Richenda being not just miles but centuries away as she stood dreamily in the Chinese Room, long, sensitive fingers running lightly over the vase she held, eyes feasting themselves on the rich red hues of the glaze with which it glowed so gorgeously.

"*Rich—en—da*!"

This time it came in a bellow; and this time it penetrated. Richenda started so violently that she came within an ace of dropping the vase. Sheer instinct made her hands tighten their grasp on it, but she had no time to replace it on the shelf whence she had lifted it, for the bellow was followed by the furious irruption of her father into the room, and she was well and truly caught. It was bad enough that she was there at all, seeing that she had been strictly forbidden ever to go there alone. What made it ten times worse was the fact that she was standing there holding his very latest acquired treasure—the valuable Khang-he vase.

"Oh, *Christmas*!" she thought to herself as she turned to face him, the vase still hugged against her.

"So here you are—*again*!" he roared. "Didn't I strictly forbid you to come here unless I was with you? Didn't I . . ." At which point his eyes fell on the vase, and he suddenly changed his tactics. "*Put—that—down*," he said in a low tone, infinitely more terrifying to his daughter than his earlier efforts. "*Put—that*—DOWN!—right in the middle of the table!"

For once in her life Richenda obeyed him implicitly. She was quaking inwardly, for her disobedience had been deliberate in even coming to the room. Twice before, he had caned her for a similar offence when he found that talking seemed to do no good. The last time, the punishment had been so severe that her hands had been sore for days. What he would do this time, she simply couldn't imagine; and yet she found it impossible to keep away. Why, oh, *why* couldn't he understand that she, too, loved the beautiful things he kept in the Chinese Room? She would never hurt them—or not so long as he didn't startle her nearly into a fit by appearing suddenly and shouting at her.

She had no time for further thought, for, once the vase was safe, he laid a heavy hand on her shoulder and marched her before him to the study where he wrote the books on Chinese ceramics which were bringing him fame among connoisseurs. A considered judgement by Professor Ambrose Fry was regarded by people who knew with deep respect.

By the time he got her there, she was feeling resentful as well as frightened. If he was as clever as everyone said, he might have taken time to think that her passion for the porcelain was an inheritance from himself and she couldn't help it. He never seemed to think of *that*!

He kicked the door to after them, and it slammed loudly which did not improve matters. He set her free, went to the swivel chair behind the big desk, and pointed to the place opposite.

"Stand there!" he said in tones that literally vibrated with rage.

Richenda took up her position with outward meekness and inward fury. Then she faced the glower he bestowed on her with head up for she was *not* going to let him see how frightened she really was. The two pairs of grey eyes, so alike in shape, colour and intelligence, met and locked, and there was silence for a few seconds. Then he spoke.

"Well? And what, pray, have you to say for yourself?"

Richenda remained silent. She could think of nothing that would mitigate her crime in his eyes. He waited. Then, seeing that he was likely to get nothing from her that way, he began his inquisition.

"I have forbidden you to go into that room unless I take you myself, haven't I?"

"Yes, Father."

"And in any case, it is a strict rule that you never—*never*, I say—handle anything there, isn't it? And you've known that most of your life?"

8

Richenda went red. "Yes, Father," she said.

"But you deliberately chose to be disobedient."

"Ye—yes, Father." Despite herself, her voice quivered a little on the last reply. She guessed she was in for it this time.

"*Why*?" he shot at her.

But though he was giving her a chance to defend herself, Richenda could think of nothing to say. In fact, she was far too scared to think clearly at all. She only wished he would cane her, or whatever it was he meant to do to her by way of punishment, and get it over.

"If you were a boy," he said slowly while his unhappy daughter squirmed inwardly and wished herself a thousand miles away, "I'd give you such a flogging as you'd remember to the last day of your life. How dare you defy me like this? You have the audacity to ignore one of my strictest rules. How *dare* you go into my private room and actually pick up and handle one of the choicest pieces of porcelain there? Do you realise that if you had dropped it you would have destroyed one of the finest specimens of its kind that I have ever even seen?"

Richenda remained silent, which was as well. He was so angry that, girl or not, if she had ventured to defend herself, she might have got the flogging. Her father glared at her until she was ready to burst into frantic yells or equally frantic tears. At last he spoke.

"Go to your room," he said, "and stay there. Don't dare to come near me until I send for you, either. And don't think you'll escape any further punishment, Miss! I'm going to make sure that in future you obey me. When I give an order, you'll do as you're told, or I'll know the reason why. Now go!"

Richenda fled, thankful for the respite, though her heart was in her mouth at the thought of what he *might* do to her. He very rarely did rouse himself to interfere with her up-bringing, preferring to leave it to Nanny and her school—she had lost her mother when she was still little more than a baby—but when he did, he did it with a vengeance. She was due to go to tea with her chum, Susan Mason, the doctor's daughter, but Susan must just think what she chose. Perhaps if her father went out later she might be able to slip down to the study and ring Susan, but that would all depend on circumstances.

She reached the haven of her room, and, as she went in, she heard the telephone bell and knew he was ringing someone. He had known she was going to the Masons' that afternoon, so perhaps he was ringing them himself to explain. What on earth would he say to them? There was never any telling where he was concerned. But it gave Richenda something more to worry about as she sat down in the wicker chair by the window.

"Oh, dear!" she thought to herself. "If only there was someone to take my part and make him see that it isn't ordinary disobedience! I just can't help it! When I see beautiful porcelain like that, I've just *got* to touch it and look at it. I get it from him—everyone says I'm as like him as can be! Why can't he see I'm like him in that, too?"

That way of thinking got her nowhere. There *was* no one to stand between them and explain her to him, since her mother was dead and her only aunt had long ago quarrelled with him, and no one knew exactly where she was now. Nanny adored her, but though she saw to it that her charge was well cared for and brought up with good manners, she had no understanding of the passion for ceramics which Richenda had indeed inherited from her father.

At one o'clock, the old woman arrived to say that the professor had told her to tell his daughter that he was out and she might come down, but she was not to leave the premises. He would be back by half-past six when she was to go to the study to learn what her punishment would be.

"And what have you been doing to need punishment?" Nanny demanded severely.

"The usual," Richenda told her laconically.

She needed no further explanation. "You've been into that room of his again in spite of all he's said to you about it? Then you're a very naughty girl, Richenda, and you deserve all you'll get. You're only a child, and a child does as she's told or takes the consequences," she scolded. "You're too old to be spanked nowadays, but your pa's got a fine rod in pickle for you, or I'm much mistaken! You go and tell him you're very sorry for all your naughtiness and maybe he'll let you off a bit."

"But I'm not sorry," Richenda returned calmly. "I just can't help it. It's part of me. And anyhow, I'll be fifteen in less than a week's time, and that's not a child. He ought to listen to me and try to understand instead of bawling——"

"Now that's quite enough!" Nanny broke in sharply. "Hold your tongue at once, Richenda, and don't expect me to stand here listening to you talking about your pa like that."

"I wasn't doing any harm in his old room," the culprit said rather more calmly.

"That's neither here nor there. He told you to stay out, and you'll stay out if you know what's good for you! Go and make yourself tidy, and then come down to the schoolroom and get your dinner. Your pa's gone off to London, he said. I'm not going to be bothered laying the dining-room table just for you. Hurry up, now!" With which valediction she stumped out of the room, leaving Richenda to wash her hands and face and tidy her hair before she ran down to the sunny back sitting-room which had been the nursery in her baby days and was now dignified by the title of schoolroom.

Nanny had the table ready, and as she passed a plate of tongue and ham and salad, she gave a further message from the professor.

"Your pa says you're to 'phone Masons' and tell them you can't go to tea with Susan this afternoon. And you're not to set foot outside the garden, so mind that. See if you can obey for once. Now hurry up and get started. I've got to go into the town this afternoon to pay the bills, and I don't want to be late and all the shops busy. I've got to oversee that Iris at the washing up. If I'm not there, she just holds the things under the tap and sets them to drain. Such laziness!"

"Will you be in for tea?" Richenda asked.

"I'll be back by half-past four—unless you and Iris between you make me late for the shops. Eat up your lettuce, Richenda."

When they had done, Nanny sailed off to the kitchen to

attend to the morals of Iris, the daily help. Richenda went off to the study to ring up the Mason house. She was lucky enough to raise Susan herself who was all that was sympathetic to her friend, though she bewailed the punishment, since it affected herself as badly as Richenda.

"Don't you worry! *This* isn't the punishment," Richenda assured her. "This is only by the way. I'm most awfully sorry, Sue. I was looking forward to coming. But Nanny says Father has a fine rod in pickle for me. Goodness only knows what it is!"

Susan, whose parents were very easy-going, repeated her sympathy, and then had to ring off. In a doctor's house you can't monopolise the telephone for a private conversation for any length of time. Richenda hung up, and went to seek a book before going off to the garden and the standing hammock, where she spent the afternoon alternately reading *Mist Over Pendle* and wondering just what ghastly punishment her father was evolving for her.

Nanny returned at half-past four and called her to tea. The meal over, Nanny sent her to change into a clean frock and make herself tidy.

"And mind and see your nails are clean," she finished. "Then you can take your book into the garden again and sit quiet till half-past six. You'll hear the church clock chiming, and if you don't, I'll call you."

Richenda did as she was told; but now that the time was so near, even the adventures of the witches of Pendle failed to hold her attention. The question of what her father meant to do to her would come bobbing up between her and the story, and she thought that half-past six would never come. When she heard the chimes from the nearby church clock, she stood up and smoothed down her skirts with hands that were suddenly clammy. Then she set off for the house, leaving the book in the hammock to take care of itself. She was met by Nanny with the information that her father had just rung up to say that he would not be at home till eight and she had better have her supper at the usual time. There was nothing for it but to go back and wait till Nanny called her at half-past seven for supper. But now the book lay where she had tossed it, and she gave herself up unreservedly to gloom.

She made such a poor supper that Nanny was secretly worried and wished that her master had seen fit to catch the earlier train. But it was twenty past eight before they heard him come in, and ten minutes more before the study bell trilled sharply through the quiet house. Nanny looked her over swiftly, and then sent her off. Richenda, now that it was upon her, simply crawled along the passage to the door and her tap was so faint that he never heard it and she had to knock again.

He heard her this time, and his voice bade her enter. She took a long breath, threw up her head and stuck out her chin, determined not to let him know how scared she was feeling, and went in. He was at his desk again, looking over something before him, and, as she shut the door, he glanced up at her.

"Come in and shut the door. Now come here. Stand there and listen to me. You're evidently getting beyond Nanny, and it's quite plain that tinpot school of yours isn't doing you much good, either. It's high time you were at a larger one where you'll learn to obey orders. I've seen Miss Hilton, and I've told her you're leaving." He stopped and glared at her.

Richenda said nothing, but inwardly she was feeling as if the bottom had dropped out of her world. Was he going to send Nanny away? But he couldn't! Who would look after the house and buy her clothes, and see to all the thousand and one things that Nanny took on so capably? And what was this about taking her away from St. Margaret's House? She had been there ever since she was seven. She and Sue had gone up the school side by side, always in the same form, always disputing in a friendly way for the top places. She knew that in another year's time they must both leave, as Miss Hilton took no girls over fifteen; but now, it seemed, she was to leave after this term. And then she found that there wasn't going to be even one last term. He had paid a term's fees in lieu of notice, and she had left!

"You need something else and you're getting it—and at once! When the new term begins, you're going to a big

13

boarding school where you'll be one of over two hundred girls, which means you'll have to toe the line pretty strictly; and that's what you need. I happened to see in *The Times* at the beginning of the week that the Head would be in London this weekend for interviews, so I went to see her, and I've made all the arrangements, so please spare me any appeals to change my mind. They'll get you nowhere!" He stopped and fished among the papers with which his desk was littered, until he found a long envelope, which he passed to her. "Here; give this to Nanny and tell her she's to get you everything on the list there. Here's a cheque for you. If it isn't enough, she can come to me for more."

Richenda grasped the envelope and cheque mechanically. She had no thought of appealing against her sentence. She was far too stunned to say anything just yet. But he had not finished what he had to say.

"I hope, Richenda, that when you have come to your senses, you'll be properly grateful to me for all I'm doing for you. When you come home at Christmas, I hope to find you a very different girl. At the moment, I expect nothing from you but unquestioning obedience. See that I get it!"

There was one thing that had to be said now, and, somehow, Richenda managed it, though it was all she could do to keep from crying, and *that* she was determined not to do in front of him.

"But—but what about half-term? Don't I come home for half-term?"

"No; it's much too far and very expensive into the bargain."

"Too *far*? But—but where *is* the school, then?"

"It's in Switzerland, in the Oberland. Now you may go. I've seen all I want of you for one day. Good night!"

Somehow Richenda contrived to reply. Somehow she got herself from the room. She went to seek Nanny, not very sure whether she was on her heels or her head. *A Swiss boarding school!* She was going among foreigners who probably didn't know a word of English, who would never play hockey or netball or cricket! And she knew no German

14

and her French was still rather of the "my-aunt-has-the-pen-of-the-gardener's-mother" variety!

Really, if her father had tried with both hands for six months on end, he could not have devised a more awful punishment for poor Richenda!

Chapter II

RICHENDA TAKES THE PLUNGE

RICHENDA stood on the platform at Victoria Station, clad in smart coat and beret of gentian blue. Beneath the coat she wore a skirt to match, and an irreproachable shirt-blouse with the tie of her new school knotted beneath the collar. Her hands were in tan gloves, and her shoes and stockings matched the gloves.

"Just a trim schoolgirl," one might have said at first glance. At the second, one would have withdrawn that. Her clothes were certainly all that they ought to be but her face, as Nanny had told her once this morning, was enough to turn any milk sour!

Her fine black brows were drawn together in an outsize in frowns. Her lips were set in a straight line, and the hand that held what the school inventory called "a night-case", gripped it as if she would like to sling it up and slug someone over the head with it.

The Professor had gone off to Harrogate the day before, to a conference of fellow connoisseurs. The pair had said farewell after breakfast, and it had been icy in the extreme. Once she had got it firmly into her head that there was to be no reprieve for her, Richenda had lapsed into a prolonged fit of what Nanny called "the black sulks". She had only opened her lips to her father when she couldn't help it. When they said good-bye, she had jerked her head back from his kiss and put her hands firmly behind her back. He had treated her *abominably* and she would never forgive him!

"Oh, very well!" he had said, "but it's to be hoped this new school of yours does something to bring you to your senses pretty quickly."

It was hardly a soothing farewell, but it was his last word to her just then. He had to hurry off to catch his train and she was left to stare sullenly out of the window and wish that she'd never been born or else that she had been born different.

Nanny had seen it all, and once her master was away, she called her nursling to account with a point and vim that had its effect.

"Richenda, you're behaving disgracefully! The master is spending a small fortune on you, and you don't deserve it, in my opinion—behaving like a naughty sulky baby. Let's have no more of it, if you please! You're going tomorrow, and at the rate you're carrying on, we're all going to be thankful to be rid of you. Stop it at once!"

She accompanied her diatribe with a sharp shake which shook Richenda out of her mood into a weepified one. She cried until poor Nanny was nearly at her wits' end to know what to do with her. However, it ended at last, and for the rest of the day the girl behaved more or less like a Christian.

As a matter of fact, she had been growing rather tired of her sulks herself. They got her nowhere, and for all the notice her father took of them, they might not have existed. She was very mournful when the Masons arrived after tea to bid her good-bye, but they contrived to cheer her up between them. The doctor produced an envelope and told her to put it into her bag and not open it until she was safely at the school. Mrs. Mason had a three-pound box of chocolates for her, and Susan had a new book. But perhaps the best of all was the news that Susan told her just as they were saying good-bye. In two more terms' time Susan herself was going to the same school, and they would be together again.

Richenda had been almost herself for the remainder of the evening, but when she came down to breakfast next morning, Nanny felt her heart go down with a thump, for the black dog was sitting firmly on her back.

"Oh, dear!" thought poor Nanny. "Whatever will the ladies that keep the school think of her if she goes on like this? But there! I dursen't say a word now. It'd only make her go off in a rage. I wish," as she watched her charge's black face, "she were young enough for me to take and give her a good spanking. It's what she needs!"

At this point, a young lady came up to them with a smile, and Nanny eyed her with approval. She was small and slight

17

and very trig and fresh-looking. When she spoke, her voice was clear and musical and very distinct.

"Good morning," she said, with another of those pretty smiles. "I think this is another new girl for the Chalet School. What is your name, dear?"

"Richenda Fry," the owner of the name muttered.

"And I'm Miss Ferrars, one of the mistresses at the school. You must be Professor Fry's daughter. Is your father here with you? We're just going to take our seats, and you'll want a last word with him I expect."

Nanny looked imploringly at her nursling, but Richenda remained dumb, so she had to explain. "The Professor has had to go to Harrogate on business, madam. I'm Richenda's old nurse—at least I was. I'm the housekeeper now. I hope you will find Richenda's things all right, madam. I think we got everything the list said. But if there's anything more she wants, the master said to ask you to write to him, and he would tell me and I'd get it and send it."

"If you've stuck to the inventory I'm sure she has everything she needs," Miss Ferrars said, laughing. "It's a most comprehensive document! Our senior mistress, Miss Derwent, is over there if you'd like to have a word with her."

Nanny shook her head. "Oh, no, madam! That will be all right. I'll just say good-bye to Richenda and then she can go with you."

Miss Ferrars nodded with another of those quick vivid smiles. "Then when Nanny has done with you, Richenda, join up with that group of girls over there, will you? They're all people of around your age, and they'll look after you." She nodded a smiling good-bye to Nanny and moved off to speak to someone else.

"That's a nice young lady," Nanny said emphatically, when she was too far off to overhear. "I hope she'll have some of the teaching of you, Richenda." She put an arm round her sulky charge. "We must say good-bye now, my dear. Be a good girl and do your best. Write to me sometimes and let me know if you want any more hankies or stockings or things like that. And now, my dear, give me a

18

kiss for good-bye and try to cheer up! It's only three months, and then you'll be coming home for the holidays—and able to talk all the foreign languages, too, I make no doubt."

She pulled down the curly red head which was well above her own, since Richenda was a long-legged creature, and bestowed a loving kiss on the sulky mouth. "God bless you, my dear, and bring you safe home to us at Christmas!"

"Good-bye!" Richenda muttered. She was in one of her worst moods and enjoying it at the moment. Nanny sighed to herself, but wisely left it to the new experiences immediately before the girl to put an end to it. She kissed her again and stepped back. Richenda suddenly dropped her case, flung both her arms round the comfortable figure in a mighty hug, and kissed her old nurse warmly. Then she picked up the case, all without a word, and went over to join on to the little group of girls Miss Ferrars had pointed out to them.

A tall girl with a thick rope of black hair dangling to her waist promptly moved over to Richenda and spoke to her. Then they were joining on to the long line of girls which was moving slowly and steadily into the train in single file.

Nanny nodded to herself as she stood watching. "A very nice happy lot they look, I must say. Let's hope Richenda settles down soon."

She gave her eyes a quick dab with her handkerchief as tears suddenly dimmed them. Richenda, glancing back as she waited for her turn to climb into the carriage, saw her and felt a sudden wild longing to break away and go rushing to her and return home with her to all the things she knew and loved. She bit her lips hard and blinked away the sudden rush of tears to her eyes. Then the girl who had taken charge of her gave her a gentle push.

"Go on, Richenda," she said. "We're holding everyone else up."

Richenda turned and clambered in. By the time she had reached the compartment she was to share with seven other people of her own age, her old nurse had vanished in the crowd. So her last link with home had gone. Then she was

19

aware that her "sheepdog", as she found later the girls called it, was speaking, and she turned to see what she wanted.

"Your case goes on the rack, Richenda, until we're well away from Victoria." She gave a sudden infectious gurgle as she added, "That's been the rule ever since Heather Clayton dropped hers between the platform and the carriage three terms ago, and there was a lovely performance before it could be fished up! Give it to me and I'll heave it up with mine, shall I?"

She took it and heaved the two cases on to the rack and then sat down, pulling Richenda down beside her. "By the way, I'm Rosamund Lilley. The rest are Joan Baker, Betty Landon, Alicia Leonard, Eve Hurrell and the two Dawbarns, Priscilla and Prudence. They're twins," she added.

Richenda looked gloomily at them. Two or three of them were exceedingly pretty, and all wore friendly expressions.

"I heard Rosamund telling you our names," Eve Hurrell said. "Tell us yours, won't you? We can't go on just calling you 'you'. It sounds most icy!"

"Richenda Fry," Richenda told her shortly.

Then she stood up, took down her case, opened it and picked out a book, after which, she returned the case to the rack and settled herself to read.

The girls glanced at each other. Was the new girl homesick and afraid to talk in case she began to weep? They had known that happen before. But as she clearly wanted to be left alone, they kindly fell in with her wishes and began to gossip among themselves about holiday doings and left her to it. Silly Richenda, having got what she wanted, promptly began to think them very unkind to leave her out.

Halfway to the coast, Eve produced a great slab of chocolate which she broke up and passed round. When it came to Richenda's turn, she eyed it stonily and said, "No, thank you." Eve raised her eyebrows, but she said nothing, merely offering it to Rosamund who accepted with gratitude.

But if Eve could hold her tongue, it was too much to expect that Prudence Dawbarn would do so. That young woman was very badly misnamed and discretion formed no part of her character. She helped herself when her turn came, gave a giggle, and then addressed Richenda directly.

"I say, are you afraid of being seasick when we cross? You needn't be. The weather forecast this morning said that everything in the garden would be lovely—or words to that effect, anyhow."

Richenda didn't trouble herself to look up from her book as she replied, "I hadn't thought about it, thank you."

Her tone was so crushing that Prudence was utterly snubbed for once in her life. She shut up and said no more. Rosamund gave her charge a quick, inquisitive look, but she changed the subject deftly by initiating a discussion about which of them was likely to go up a form this term and in the interest of it, they forgot Richenda who sat turning the pages of her book without taking in anything of what she was supposed to be reading.

"I won't, for one," Prudence said with certainty. "I was seventeenth in form last term and eighteenth in exams. It's Inter V for me again this year. But Pris was ninth and seventh, so she's safe for Vb and we'll be parted, alas!"

Betty giggled. "Well, that'll be some relief to the staff and prees!" she remarked.

"What on earth do you mean?" Priscilla herself demanded with some heat.

"Only that *one* of you in a form ought to be enough for anyone," Betty explained sweetly. "I wonder if all three of the Maynards will go up, by the way?"

"Len and Con for certain," Rosamund said. "Len was bracketed second with Jo Scott and Con was eighth. They're safe for a remove."

"What about young Margot?" Eve queried. "Thirteenth, wasn't she? You know, she ought to be a lot better than that. She's got heaps of brains."

"Yes, but she still doesn't use them all the time," Rosamund said. "Len and Con work steadily, but you can't always rely on Margot. She does the maddest things on occasion. Anyhow," she added cheerfully, "she's just a kid still."

"So are Len and Con, if you come to that," Joan Baker put in. "Not fourteen till November, are they?"

"November fifth," Rosamund agreed. Then she giggled. "Len once told me that her mother always says their arrival was her big bang on that day."

The others joined in her giggles and, despite herself, Richenda, who had been listening with all her ears, nearly gave herself away by gasping aloud. She had heard of triplets, of course, but she had never met any before. Were there really triplets in this school? How simply weird. And there were twins, too, because Prudence and Priscilla were twins. Rosamund Lilley had said so. She began to wonder about the Maynard trio. Were they all as alike to look at as the Dawbarns?

She stole a brief glance through her lashes at the pair sitting side by side. They were very alike with wavy brown hair, hazel eyes and short, uptilted faces. She fancied it would take her some time to know them apart. *Three* girls as alike would be something of a problem. But at least, as she now realised, one part of her difficulties had melted away. There were a tremendous number of English girls in the school so she supposed they would be allowed to speak their own language occasionally. *That* was something to be thankful for!

By this time, the others had all produced sweets or chocolate. They were punctilious in offering her a share, but she refused everything. She was *not* going to make friends in this ghastly school! Susan would remain her only friend—and every minute she was going further and further away from Susan. She glanced down at her watch. St. Margaret's began today and by this time, they would all be hard at it. How was Sue getting on? What new girls were there? Had Miss Coulson *really* left? There had been rumours about it last term, but no one seemed to know for certain. It would be ages before she could hear anything. She had very vague ideas about how long it would take a letter from home to reach the Görnetz Platz, but at least a week, she felt sure! Oh, *why* must her father send her right away from everything and everyone she loved just because she hadn't been able to resist the Chinese Room and that wretched Khang-he vase.

If she had been alone, this was where she would probably have burst into tears. As it was, she swallowed hard and concentrated on her book, deliberately shutting her ears on the gay chatter that was going on round her.

Presently Rosamund, feeling guiltily that the new girl was being left out, spoke to her again. "Have you ever travelled by this line before, Richenda?"

"No, never," Richenda replied briefly.

"It's rather decent country, isn't it?" Rosamund went on perseveringly. "Kent *is* a pretty county, don't you think?"

"I don't know anything about it," Richenda told her, still in that brusque manner. Her tone added, "And I don't want to, so let me alone!"

Rosamund gave it up. If Richenda wouldn't talk, she wouldn't talk and there was nothing to be gained by trying to make her. No more than anyone else did she like being snubbed so downrightly. A question from Alicia Leonard gave her the excuse. She replied to it and Richenda was left to herself once more.

Presently, there came the sound of light footsteps and a tall girl looked in on them to be hailed by a delighted chorus of greeting from the others, who called her "Mary-Lou", and rained questions on her.

Mary-Lou leaned up against the door into the corridor, beaming benignly on them all. Richenda glanced up at her long enough to realise that she was exceedingly attractive, tall and slim, with a shapely head covered by a fuzz of brown curls that were full of golden gleams. Her very blue eyes were dancing behind their long fringe of black, up-curled lashes. She had a perfect complexion, and her smiling mouth was beautifully cut and her best feature. She replied to their vociferous greeting in clear, bell-like tones.

"Glad to see you all again! Hallo! A new girl! Welcome to our midst! What's your name?"

Richenda had to look up at this. Nanny's rigid training in good manners held, even in her present black mood. "Richenda Fry," she said.

"Richenda? What a jolly pretty name! And absolutely uncommon! I've never met it before. Well, Richenda, I'm

23

one of the prefects. If ever you want a spot of help, mind you come along and ask me and I'll do what in me lies. That's one thing we prefects are for—besides making all you people toe the line!" she added with an infectious grin at the others, who broke into loud protests—all but Prudence Dawbarn, who looked sheepish and said nothing. "Well, I'm just going the rounds to remind everyone that Dover's getting near and you must make sure you have all your possessions handy. There isn't any too much time between the train and the boat, and if we miss it, we'll hold up all the people in Paris. You can guess how dearly we should all be loved if we did *that*! She flashed another grin round and added, "You have been *warned*!" The she removed herself from the doorway and vanished into the next-door compartment.

The younger girls set to work at once, rather to Richenda's amazement. She had expected them to take their time about preparations. But in five minutes' time, everyone was sitting with her night-case on her knee, beret pulled on, any other impedimenta such as umbrella, hockey-stick, raincoat, leaning against her and all ready to leave the train on the word. Rosamund had seen to it that she herself was as ready as the others and her book had been put into the case.

When they had done everything, they sat waiting, and the talk turned on the prefects—and especially Mary-Lou. Richenda gathered that she was something rather particular in the school. The girls all spoke of her with affection and admiration, even if they criticised her.

"Think she's slated for Head Girl this year?" Alicia demanded presently.

"I expect so," Betty returned. "It'll be either her or Hilary—or there's Vi Lucy, of course," she added.

"It won't be Vi, anyhow," Eve said with decision.

"How d'you know that?" Priscilla Dawbarn asked. "She could do it all right. She just like Julie and Betsy, and look what decent Head Girls they both were. I like Vi. I think she'd made a jolly decent Head Girl. She's got what it takes."

"I'm not disputing that," Eve said calmly. "All the same, she won't be it this year. She hasn't been a full-blown prefect for a year—only last term when Amy Dunne left. Mary-Lou and Hilary have. When those two are available, the Abbess and Bill aren't very likely to fall back on someone who's had only a term of prefecting.

"And if you think it'll be Hilary, you've another guess coming," big Joan Baker shoved her oar in.

"Why ever not?" Prudence demanded, wide-eyed.

"Well, won't she be slated for Games? She was Second Games last year and she's the best all-rounder of the prefects. If you ask me, I'd say there's no question about it—it'll go to Mary-Lou. She'll be jolly good, too."

"She'll always be too jolly on the spot, you mean!" Prudence said gloomily.

"Don't go making a silly ass of yourself and then it won't matter to you," Betty told her briskly. "The more on the spot she is, the better, I should say. We've our own fair share of demons among the Middles."

"Listen to the pot calling the kettle black!" Eve giggled. "I've always heard you were never a little angel yourself in your Middles days!"

"That," Betty said sedately, "is why I know what Middles need in the way of a Head Girl. I hope it *is* Mary-Lou. She'll make a real go of it."

"You're quite right, Bets." This was the thoughful Rosamund. "I don't know how she does it, but she seems to be able to see all round everyone else's point of view almost before they get there themselves. And she's always just and kind and helpful."

"She's too jolly on the spot for me," Prudence reiterated gloomily.

Richenda took no part in the chatter, of course, though she listened with all her ears. In spite of her determination to loathe everyone and everything connected with her new school, she couldn't help liking the prefect who, to judge by the gossip of the rest, was going to hold one of the most coveted posts in the school.

"I don't know what's wrong with me!" she told herself crossly. "I *won't* like her! I won't like any of them! I loathe the place and the people and everything and I'll go *on* loathing them! And Father's a cruel pig to treat me like this!"

The result was that when she followed the others on to the boat, Francie Wilford, who had travelled in the next-door compartment, stared at her with interest, and then demanded of Betty Landon and Priscilla Dawbarn if they knew just why that new girl looked as if she had committed a murder and didn't know what to do with the body?

Chapter III

NEW EXPERIENCES FOR RICHENDA

"HAVE you all got your cases and other oddments ready?" Miss Ferrars demanded as the motor-coach in which Richenda was sitting beside Rosamund Lilley swung round a wide curve in the road. "Make sure, please. We're terribly late, thanks to that wash-out, and the men have to get the coaches back to Interlaken tonight. You've all got to be ready to pour out the moment it's our turn, and waste not one moment! Prunella and Clare, just see that the racks are quite cleared, will you?"

Two Seniors rose from their seats and examined the luggage-racks from end to end before reporting that they were clear. The girls had hurriedly collected all their belongings and were all sitting looking very alert, and very thankful that their ordeal was so nearly over. For it *had* been an ordeal. Usually, they got into the train at the Gare du Nord in Paris, changed at Basle for the Berne express, and left the train there for the big motor-coaches always chartered by the school at the beginning and end of term, without any major incident happening. On this occasion, however, fate had seen fit to vary the programme.

They had reached Basle without any trouble, though Richenda, for one, had felt very muzzy as she clambered out of the train and met the chill air of six o'clock on a September morning. There was time for coffee and rolls in the station restaurant before they took their places in the train for Berne and then—it happened!

The express runs from Basle to Berne with about two stops. On this occasion, however, they were held up at Meinsburg where information had been received, that thanks to recent heavy rains there had been a landslide, and part of the embankment had collapsed ten minutes previously. All trains in the area were being stopped and sent round, where possible, to Solothurn. Theirs would be backed there and thence they must go by a very roundabout route to Berne.

27

The staff had looked very blue at this. It meant at least two hours added to their journey. *That* meant that they would reach the Görnetz Platz somewhere about twenty o'clock as the startled Richenda overheard them all saying, instead of eighteen. As soon as a telephone was available, Miss Derwent, head of the party, sent little Miss Andrews flying to ring up the school and warn them of what had happened. She only just managed it. In fact, the train was on the move out of Solothurn station as she scrambled up the high steps to the carriage where she was caught by Mlle Lenoir, one of the junior music mistresses, and yanked to safety to a chorus of shrieks from the girls.

The Seniors were mostly old enough to realise what difficulties this diversion would make, and some of them grumbled over the extra length of the journey. The Middles and Juniors thought it huge fun—then. Later, as they became more and more stiff and cramped, they began to growl on their own account.

The change to the motor-coaches, when at long last they reached Berne, roused them all, but was not much help where comfort was concerned. They were much more cramped than the railway carriages, and it had been a fairly silent and thoroughly tired-out set of girls for the last hour of the run through the mountains, going higher and higher as they went. At last, they reached a level road which ran through two or three tiny villages where lights twinkled at them from the chalet windows and very few people seemed to be about. By this time it was dusk and they could see very little. Then, as they swung round a wide curve in the road, Rosamund nudged Richenda, who was nearly asleep, and pointed to the left where a tall bulk loomed up, with lights showing at several windows.

"That's Freudesheim where the Maynards live," she said. "It's next door to the school, so we shan't be long now."

Richenda roused with difficulty. "Oh?" she said, little interest in her voice.

Rosamund gave it up for the time being. During the whole of the journey she had loyally done her best to make the new girl feel welcome among them. She had tried to bring her

28

charge into the gay chatter which had enlivened the first part of the journey. She had pressed sweets and magazines on her, and done every single thing she could think of to help Richenda over what she and the rest had diagnosed as an extra-violent case of home-sickness. *Nothing* seemed to have the slightest effect. Richenda refused the corner seat Rosamund self-sacrificingly offered her, declined sweets and papers, and only opened her lips when she was asked direct questions. She had asked none herself, though her "sheepdog" had begged her to ask anything she wanted to know, and had tried to impart various pieces of information about life at the Chalet School. For about the tenth time since they had left Victoria station, Rosamund decided disgustedly that you couldn't do a thing with her.

By this time it was quite dark. They turned in at some gates and rolled up a short drive, and Richenda couldn't avoid seeing the girls from the coach immediately before theirs, marching steadily and smartly round the building which was glowing with lights from every window, swing round and be lost to sight. Even as their own vehicle slowed up, the other moved off, and they came to a halt before a wide door where a tall, slim woman in her mid-thirties, with the light from the lamp in the wide entrance shining on her fair hair, waited to direct them.

The girls greeted her with delighted cries of, "Oh, Miss Dene!" and Richenda wondered if she was one of the mistresses. Then she remembered that Rosamund had told her that Miss Dene was the school secretary, and an Old Girl herself. She was evidently regarded as a good friend by everyone judging by the way they greeted her. She replied to their clamour laughingly, but remained firm all the same.

"We'll be seeing plenty of each other during the next three months or so. It's terribly late, and there are two coaches after yours. Hurry up and get out of the way as fast as you can. Splasheries first and then to your common rooms until the gong sounds for Abendessen—and that won't be many minutes. There's no time for gossip now. We can talk later."

They calmed down at once, and each clutched her possessions and set off. Rosamund forgivingly saw to it that

Richenda went with them, and three minutes later, that young woman found herself entering a side-door and being steered along a passage to a long, narrow room, with pegs on the two side-walls, a peg-stand running down the centre, two big windows with toilet basins beneath, and at the far end, lockers built right up to the ceiling. This, she was informed, was the new Splashery for the three fifth forms. A door beside the lockers led into a much smaller room which contained four more toilet basins and more lockers. Rosamund made straight for the wall opposite the main door and hunted along it.

"Here we are! This is your peg, Richenda, next door to mine." She turned to the girl on the other side of Richenda. "Hello, Primrose! I didn't see you on the train! This is Richenda Fry, a new girl. If I'm not ready in time, show her where her locker is, will you?"

Primrose, a fair, pretty girl with hair as rampantly curly as Richenda's own, and a wicked twinkle in her blue eyes, nodded. "O.K. Someone's on the yell for you, Ros! Better scram! I'll see to—*what* did she call you?" turning to Richenda as Rosamund vanished among the mob.

"Richenda Fry," the owner of the name replied curtly.

"Gosh! That's a new one on me!" Primrose was frankly slangy at this end of the term. "Well, better get cracking. We haven't a moment to spare and Matey is the outside of enough when it comes to being late for anything!"

With this piece of advice, Primrose yanked off her coat and beret and hung them up, tucked her gloves into a pocket and proceeded to unstrap her case and produce slippers and towel. She kept one eye on Richenda to make sure that she followed suit, and when both stood up in their slippers, Primrose tucked a hand through the arm of the new girl, who by this time, wasn't sure if she were on her heels or her head, and steered her through the throng to the lockers.

"Now, let's see! Oh, here you are! This is yours— "R. Fry"—and here's mine just below. This one next to you belongs to Ros—and here she comes! Hello, Ros! Here's your locker all safe. Let's shove our shoes in and get washed and clear out of this place. It sounds like a looney-bin!"

Rosamund grinned. *"That'll* soon stop, thank goodness! Don't be scared, Richenda. Tomorrow, rules come into full force, and you're either silent in the Splashery or talk in whichever language for the day it is."

Richenda stared. What on earth did she mean? There wasn't time to ask, however, even if she wasn't still determined to make no advances to anyone. Primrose and Rosamund saw to that. They marched her back to her peg to get her towel and then to one of the wash basins where, by main force of wriggling and pushing, they contrived to make places for themselves and were able to wash.

Richenda thankfully splashed her hot face with the cold, velvety-feeling water and then set to scrubbing her hands which were filthy. Primrose gave her a matey grin as she, too, did her best to remove the dirt.

"Filthy stuff they use on the steam trains abroad, isn't it? Soft coal it is, and no matter how careful you are, you just can't help getting dirty. Baths at bedtime, though—unless they decide that we're too late and we'd better wait till the morning. Got your comb handy? Better tidy your wig. It looks *wild*!"

Richenda had forgotten her comb, but Primrose offered hers when she had reduced her fair curls to something like order. Once it had been run through the ruddy mop she began to feel better and ready for her supper—if that was what Miss Dene had meant by that weird word. Foreign, she supposed. Would they have foreign food as well? Would they have——Richenda handed back the comb, hastily searching her memory for any foreign foods of which she had heard. Only one came and she actually forgot her vow of silence long enough to ask Primrose if they would be having sauerkraut for their meal. Primrose first stared at her blankly, and then went off into fits of laughter.

Richenda stared at her offendedly. "I don't see anything to laugh at," she said stiffly.

"Sorry," Primrose gasped, "but it sounded so awful! We don't go in for exotic dishes of that kind! Whatever else we have for Abendessen, it certainly won't be that! Much more

31

likely to be cold meat and salad and fruit and cream. We'll know in a minute or two."

She steered Richenda through the crowd, along the passage, down another and into a third where she opened a door halfway along and ushered her charge into the Senior common room where Rosamund was waiting near the door.

"Oh, there you are!" she exclaimed, coming to claim her "lamb". "This is our common room, Richenda, where we spend our free time when we can't go out. Rather jolly, isn't it?"

Before Richenda could do more than glance round, a deep, booming sound rang out and at once everyone stopped chattering and hurried to form into line by the door. Two of the elder girls who were clearly prefects, appeared and took command and they marched out "decently and in order", to quote Rosamund later, back down the corridor, along another and so into a very long room which Primrose, just behind her, hissed over her shoulder was the "Speisesaal".

They took their places behind the pretty peasant chairs standing along the sides of the lengthy refectory tables which ran down the room in three rows with another across the top of the room. When everyone was present, a tall, stately woman in a green dress said a short Latin Grace in a deep, musical voice which had something of the quality of the 'cello in it. They all sat down and plates of cold, stuffed veal were placed before them.

Richenda sat looking round and taking in all she saw. And it was quite a good deal. She filled a page of writing pad with her description of the room when she wrote to Nanny on Sunday. The tables were spread with gaily-checked cloths and they all had napkins to match. The glasses at each place were of different colours—ruby, sapphire, emerald, topaz, garnet—and under the electric light, they glowed like the jewels they resembled in colour. Down the centre were great platters of peasant ware, as gay as the cloths, and piled high with delectable salad. Salad dressing was in glass jugs which matched their tumblers. Hand-woven baskets held crisp rolls on which they spread ivory butter, firm and sweet. The chairs delighted her, too, with her passionate love of colour. They were of white wood, enamelled and varnished cream, and on the back of each was painted a posy of Alpine flowers, all different. Later, she heard that the Senior art classes were responsible for the floral decoration.

She was so absorbed in it all that her neighbours had to jog her or her plate would still have been full when the Head signalled to the maids beside the hatch to change the plates. Thanks to Rosamund and Primrose, however, she did pick up her fork, and then came a new thrill. She had never tasted anything more delicious than that veal.

"What is it?" she whispered to Primrose, since Rosamund was talking to Joan Baker at the moment.

"Kalbsbraten," Primrose said solemnly, though her eyes danced wickedly.

"Kalbsbraten? What, exactly is that? I don't know any German."

"Roast veal, my child. Karen does it gorgeously, doesn't she? Karen—the cook, of course. She's one of the foundation stones of this establishment. She was with the school when it was in Tirol—ages and ages ago."

"Oh, goody!" broke from the girl sitting at Primrose's right hand. "Bricelets! I do love them!"

"Oh, we all know what your middle name is, Emmy," Primrose said with a chuckle. "Sugar-baby! Not that I don't like them myself," she added as her plate was passed to her.

Richenda tasted her portion cautiously. Then she set to work to finish it. It consisted of a square, sweeted wafer, fried in olive oil and sprinked with sugar and, as she told Sue Mason in one of her letters, luscious beyond words.

As the meal was ending, a bell rang through the room and at once the hum of chatter and laughter ceased, and everyone turned expectantly to the top table where the lady in green had risen and was smiling at them.

"One moment, girls," she said. "It is very late, thanks to the accident to the railway line. I will leave my usual talk till after Prayers tomorrow morning. You all have— or ought to have—all you need for the night in your night-cases. As soon as you have finished and cleared the tables, you are to go straight to Prayers—Protestants to Hall and Catholics to the gym, as usual. After Prayers, you go upstairs to bed—everyone! You must all be very tired and we can leave everything until the morning. I'll just take this opportunity of welcoming every one back to school and saying that I hope all the new girls will settle in among us as soon as possible and be very happy with us. In the morning, when Prayers are over, you will unpack and those not required by Matron first will come to Miss Dene in the office to report. There has been no time for it this evening.

"Now that is all for the moment. Finish your meal and don't loiter over clearing the tables. The Juniors are all very sleepy, I know, and the rest of you will welcome your comfortable beds after last night in the train." She smiled at them again and sat down, and they set to work to clear their plates and glasses before the bell at the high table rang again and they stood for grace.

When grace ended, each girl seized her plate, glass, spoon and fork and went to pile them on one of the big, three-tiered trolleys waiting. As each trolley was filled, a prefect pulled up wire sides which kept everthing safe, and they were left for the maids to wheel out later. They had to take their napkins and put them in one of the drawers of a great armoire built into the wall at one side and the prefects at the head and foot of the tables folded up the cloths and added them to their own drawer—one for each table. When it was all done, the girls went to join one of two long lines forming at the head of the room behind the high table which the staff had left as soon as grace had been said.

Rosamund turned to her charge and asked, "Which are you—C. of E. or R.C.?"

"Why—C. of E., I suppose," Richenda said doubtfully.

"Don't you know?" Rosamund asked involuntarily.

"Yes, it's C. of E. all right."

"Then join on to this line after me." Rosamund led the way and presently someone said, "March!" and they all marched quietly down the corridors and into an enormous room with a dais at the top end. On the dais stood a lectern, a beautiful Willam and Mary chair in carved walnut and cane-work, and behind these, a semi-circle of ordinary chairs. A piano stood at one side and a mistress was already seated at it, turning the pages of a hymn book on the desk.

Richenda might have resolved to talk as little as possible, but she was only human, and by this time she was nearly bursting with questions. She conveniently forgot her resolve and turned to Rosamund as soon as they were sitting on one of the long, green-painted forms which filled the upper part of the room.

"Who was that that spoke at supper?"

"The Head, of course—at least, *one* of the Heads. That's Miss Annersley. She's Head here and Miss Wilson is Head at St. Mildred's. But they work in together most of the time. This school has two Heads."

"St. Mildred's? Which is that?"

"The finishing branch where most girls go for their last year. But it's all in the prospectus. Didn't you see it?" Rosamund demanded, startled.

"No," Richenda said with a sudden guilty memory of her blank refusal even to look at it. She was rather sorry about that now.

"Oh, well," Rosamund said, inwardly delighted that this new girl seemed to be coming round a little, "you'll soon know all about it. Ask me anything you want to know and I'll tell you if I can."

"Well, why do we have **two** lots of Prayers?" Richenda demanded.

"Because we have nearly as many Catholics and Pro-testants—or *quite* as many I should think, nowadays. When Bill—er—I mean Miss Wilson—is here, she takes Prayers for the Catholics. When she isn't, Mlle de Lachennais does. It mostly *is* her. Miss Wilson has to be with her own girls at St. Mildred's as a rule. Miss Annersley always takes us unless she's away or engaged."

"Do you always call Miss Wilson 'Bill'?" Richenda asked curiously; and a deep red flooded Rosamund's clear skin.

"We oughtn't, of course. But she always has been, they say."

"Then what do you call Miss Annersley?"

35

But before Rosamund could answer, a bell pealed out from somewhere overhead, and even the very quiet talk which had been going on among the girls was hushed on the instant. Prefects appeared with piles of prayer-books which they handed out. Mary-Lou appeared on the platform to announce, "The beginning of term hymn!" in her clear ringing tones. Then the mistress at the piano began to play softly—a Bach prelude, if Richenda had only known—and everyone sat very quietly.

"Almost like one of our Meetings," Richenda thought as she glanced round.

Her father was, of course, a Quaker, but she herself had mostly gone to the parish church with Nanny who was staunch Church of England. But she had attended a few Quakers' Meetings and now once more she began to feel the same hush which had always pervaded them. She had yet to learn that this interval of peace was intended to help the girls to a devout mood before Prayers actually began.

The top door opened and the mistresses entered quietly, headed by Miss Annersley, who wore her M.A. gown flung over her pretty jade-green dress. She took up her stand behind the lectern and the staff went quietly to their seats before Miss Lawrence, at the piano, modulated from Bach into the hymn, which was sung with gusto by everyone. When it ended, they sat down and Mary-Lou, looking for once in her life rather discomposed, read the parable of the Talents, after which they all knelt while Miss Annersley repeated two or three collects, led them in the *Our Father* which belongs to all Christians; then *Gentle Jesus* for the little ones and, finally, the lovely old Antiphon, *Oh, God, keep us waking, watch us sleeping that awake, we may watch with Thee and asleep, we may rest in peace*." It was new to Richenda, but she listened as Rosamund and Primrose on either side of her repeated it devoutly, and she like it immensely.

The blessing followed and they all remained on their knees for a few moments. Then they stood up and Miss Annersley wished them all goodnight and sweet sleep. The girls returned the wish and then, to the tune of a quiet march, they left Hall and went upstairs to the dormitories, Richenda keeping close to Rosamund who had already consulted dormitory lists and found that her charge was in Pansy with her.

There was no talking on the stairs, but once they were in the dormitory, Rosamund spoke again. "This is Pansy. Let's see which is your cubey. Here you are!" as she led the way along the narrow aisle made by curtains at one side and the green wall of the room at the other. "This cubey is Betty's and I'm on your other side. The rest of us are Heather Clayton, Len Maynard, the eldest of the Maynard triplets— eldest by half-an-hour," she added with a sudden chuckle, "and two new girls, Odette Mercier and Carmela Walther. Half a tic till I see who's our pree."

But before she could move, the curtains of the big cubicle at one end of the dormitory were swept apart, and a girl of their own age in dressing-gown and bedroom slippers with her thick pigtail of reddish hair twisted up on top of her head appeared, towel in one hand and sponge bag in the other.

"Jo Scott!" Rosamund exclaimed. "Are *you* our dormy pree this term?"

"Looks like it," Jo said with a grin. "You're no more surprised than I am, Ros. But now our one and only Mary-Lou has the Head Girl's room, someone had to take her place, and believe it or not, they've pitched on *me*!"

"They might have done worse,"commented Betty, poking a tousled head between her own curtains. "Supposing they'd chosen ME!"

"Don't you worry!" A long-legged individual with curling chestnut hair tumbling about her to her waist, dashed into the fray. "No one on *this* staff is either blind, deaf, or crackers! Hello, Ros! Haven't had a chance to see you before. And there's not going to be much chance now," she continued, pushing the heavy waves of hair out of her eyes. "Lights Out will go in precisely twenty minutes, so I'd advise you to get cracking. Who's this?" She turned a frankly interested gaze on Richenda and beamed at her.

"This is Richenda Fry," Rosamund said. "Richenda, this is Len, one of the Maynard triplets. Now come on into your

37

cubey. You can talk tomorrow. There isn't time now. This peg is for your dressing-gown and this is your bureau. Mirror here and you keep your brush and comb in this little locker affair beneath. Your clothes go into those drawers—all but your frocks and coats and so on. You have three pegs and hangers in the closet at the far end for those. I'll help you fold your counterpane and then I must fly. I'll come to show you the bathroom in five minutes, so mind you're ready. I'm just next door if you want me." And having instituted the new girl into her cubicle, she scurried out, and to judge by the sounds, undressed in a frantic hurry.

Richenda was so sleepy by this time that she was yawning almost continuously. She was unaccustomed to lengthy journeys and she had had a whole bunch of new experiences on top of that, so small wonder that she was weary! She tossed off her clothes and contrived to be ready when Rosamund arrived to take her to the bathroom. She washed her face and hands, but nearly forgot to brush her teeth, so drowsy was she. However, she remembered in time and was ready when Rosamund appeared to escort her back to the dormitory.

"Finish undressing, and do your hair," Rosamund said. "The bell for private prayers will ring in less than ten minutes and it'll be lights out five minutes after that. Good night, Richenda. I hope you'll sleep well."

"Good night," Richenda mumbled, repressing a yawn with difficulty. "Thanks for all your help."

"That's all right," Rosamund said. "When I was new I was helped, and next term it may be your turn. We all do it. Good night!"

She slipped through the dividing curtains and Richenda was left to discard the rest of her clothes and pull on her pyjamas. A bell rang just as she finished buttoning the jacket and she contrived to remember about the prayers. But though she knelt at the side of her bed, it is to be feared that they got all mixed up and when the second bell rang, she just dived into bed under the sheet and blankets and pretty, pansy-powdered couvrepied. Then she fell down, down, down until she was drowned in sleep and knew nothing more till the morning.

Chapter IV

In Form vb

RICHENDA slept like a log all night. She was roused at half-past six next morning by the loud pealing of a bell. Still half-asleep, she bounced up in bed and stared wildly round her. Where on earth was she? As the fog left her brain, she began to remember. She also took in the appearance of her cubicle and a spontaneous exclamation of, "Oh, what a *pretty* room!" was jerked out of her before she could stop it.

A pleased voice from behind the curtains on her right replied at once. "Yes, rather nifty, isn't it? Sorry I can't come in to you, but visiting is strictly forbidden unless it's an emergency. And talking of emergencies, we're both likely to run head-on into one if we don't get up at once! Matey's dead nuts on punctuality, let me tell you!"

A thud followed this speech, showing that Betty had suited her actions to her words, and Richenda felt she had better imitate her. She threw back her bedclothes, swung her feet to the floor, made a long arm and grabbed her dressing-gown from the hook where it seemed to have found its own way. She had a hazy memory of tossing it down somewhere last night. She was not to know that Rosamund had peeped in on her last thing, and seeing the mess in her cubicle, had broken rules and tidied it up.

As she pulled on the blue gown and the front curtains swayed apart Rosamund's black head was poked between them.

"You're up! Oh, good! I just called in to tell you that you're after me on the bath-list, so be ready to fly when I come back. There are people after you, you know. Strip your bed while you wait—Betty or someone will show you if you're not sure——"

"I will, Ros," said Len Maynard's pretty voice behind her.

"Oh, good for you, Len! Thanks a lot! You'll be all right with Len, Richenda." The black head was withdrawn as Rosamund scuttled off to the bathroom and Richenda was left to wonder why someone should have to show her how to strip a bed. Nanny had taught her that years ago!

There came the patter of light feet and Len Maynard peered in at her. "Shall I show you what to do, Richenda? Matey's rather sticky about beds being stripped in the one way she thinks best."

Richenda took firm hold of her wits. "Thanks, but I *can* strip a bed," she replied. And she pulled off couvrepied and blankets and flung them over the back of a chair, followed them with her sheets and pillows and finally turned the mattress over the foot of the bed.

Len watched here approvingly until she came to the mattress. There, she interfered. "I hope you don't mind me telling you, but Matey makes us hump it up in the middle— like this—to let the air pass under it." She "humped" the mattress and then grinned at the new girl. "Matey insists on doing it this way and it's always best to fall in with her ideas. She's a perfect poppet when she likes; but get across her and you know *all* about it!"

"Len Maynard! What are you doing in someone else's cubey?" Jo Scott's voice demanded firmly from the aisle. Then she came in, looking well-washed and glowing, with her mane of reddish hair beginning to tumble down from the screwed-up knot into which she had tied it on top of her head.

"Only showing Richenda the way Matey likes us to strip our beds," Len explained. "She doesn't need any showing, really, except about the mattress. Here comes Ros! Grab your things and scram, Richenda! There isn't time to breathe in the mornings here! D'you know where to go, by the way?"

Richenda nodded as she snatched up her belongings and shot off down the dormitory, urged to instant flight by everyone else's insistence. Betty Landon came flying behind her as if wolves were after her. Clearly dilly-dallying was *not* encouraged here!

As they met at the bathroom door, Betty panted, "Cold or lukewarm, but *not* hot! And for pity's sake don't splash or you'll have it to clear up!"

She entered the cubicle next door to the one Richenda had used the night before, and judging by the sounds, plunged straight into her bath. Richenda found that Rosamund had left the cold water running for her. She brushed her teeth while the bath filled and then, with the remembrance of Betty's warning, got in, gasping a little under the sting of the icy mountain water. A quick splash and she was out again, towelling herself hard. Even so, she heard Betty leaving when she herself was only half-dry. She dropped the towel, pulled on her night-clothes, and having turned on the tap for the next person, gathered up her things and headed for the dormitory once more, feeling fully refreshed. She had to finish drying in her cubicle, but by the time she was in her well-cut skirt and shirt-blouse with the school tie knotted smartly beneath the collar, her curls gleaming from a hard brushing, and everything about her spick and span, she was glowing and warm and her rather pale cheeks were flushed with pink, partly from her haste, partly as a result of her icy tub.

Jo Scott, making the rounds to see that all the cubicles were in order, stared.

"Well," she said crisply, "I know Switzerland is the place for good complexions, but I should say you'd beaten the record for collecting one early! Let me see your cubey. It's one of my jobs to keep tab on tidiness. Yes, you've done everything. Don't forget to take your blazer downstairs when we go. You'll need it for the walk after Frühstück——"

"After—*what* did you say?" Richenda gasped, nearly stunned by the new word and not very sure what awful thing it might imply.

"Frühstück—breakfast, in other words," Jo told her with a matey grin. "It's German for it. So if you've never learnt any before, there's one word for you!"

"I don't know any German whatsoever," Richenda confided in her, forgetting that she had meant to be very chilly and reserved with everyone. But how were you to remember a thing like that when you have to do everything on the run the whole time?

"Oh, well, you'll soon pick up enough to get around

with. *I* did; and if I could, you can. You're no dud, to judge by your looks." After which stately compliment, which caused Richenda to go a rich purple, Jo moved on to see what Odette Mercier and Carmela Walther were doing.

By this time everyone was back from the bathrooms, and most of them were frantically finishing their dressing. Being blessed with short curly hair which needed only a vigorous brushing to bring up the gloss, Richenda was ready fairly quickly. She was standing before her mirror, twisting and turning to make sure that her skirt and blouse were accurately together, when the bell rang again. Jo Scott's voice sounded at once: "Prayers, everyone!"

Richenda slid to her knees with a startled feeling. Nanny had taught her to say prayers night and morning, but it must be admitted that more often than not she omitted the morning session. She had a bad habit of reading while she was dressing. This slowed her down and left no time for prayers if she were to be at the breakfast table when the gong sounded. Professor Fry was insistent on punctuality and it was rarely that Richenda transgressed against that rule. Here, she reflected as she buried her head in her hands, they didn't take any chances when they had a bell rung for it.

Five minutes later, the relentless peal came again and everyone left her cubicle, the old hands flinging up their curtains over the crossbars to let the fresh morning air circulate freely through the room. Richenda instantly imitated them and so did another of the new girls, Carmela Walther. Odette Mercier, who seemed to be a mooner, was still fiddling with her tie and when Len Maynard looked in to see how she was getting on, she was discovered to be on the verge of tears. Len took her in hand at once; knotted the tie, pinned it with the little moziac brooch meant for the job, threw up the curtains and hustled Odette out of her cubicle and into line with the others all in about two minutes. Richenda felt mentally breathless and Odette looked as if she wasn't very sure which end of her was uppermost!

"Oh, mais c'est tout effroyable!" Odette moaned; and most of the others grinned.

"Vous—er—vous accoutumerez tôt," Jo said encouragingly; but Odette looked doubtful.

Then Betty led the way and they all filed demurely after her along the corridor, down the stairs and into the Senior common room. Richenda glanced at her watch. It was exactly half-an-hour since she had got up.

"What do we do now?" she asked Rosamund.

"Usually we go to our form rooms and look over any lessons we aren't sure of. In the summer, we may go out and work in the form gardens if we like. Music people have practice, of course. But there isn't any prep and no one knows yet about the music timetable," Rosamund explained.

"Then what *do* we do?" Richenda persisted.

"Oh, just mooch about for the time being until the gong sounds for Frühstück," Joan Baker butted in to say.

"I see. Thank you," Richenda replied, the old coldness back in her voice and manner. She was a fastidious young woman and so far she had no liking for this girl with her assured, rather sophisticated air and her cheaply pretty face.

Joan flushed and Rosamund spoke quickly. "Are you taking music, Richenda?"

"No; I am not really musical," Richenda replied. Then, for she had decided that she must at least be polite, she added, "Do you?"

Rosamund shook her head. "I hadn't started when I came here and everyone said I had so much to make up on languages and maths that I'd better not tackle anything more. But I'd love to try my hand at a fiddle sometime," she added wistfully. "It's my favourite instrument. However, that'll have to wait. You see," she went on, "before I came here, I went to a government school and I found I was very much behind most of the others in some subjects."

Richenda was too well-bred to make any remark about this and Len Maynard, who had overheard, laughed. "If it's a fiddle you want, Ros, you can have a shot on mine any time. I'll show you how to hold it and make the notes. Why on earth didn't you tell me sooner? You might have been doing quite a bit at it this last two or three terms. Your French and German are as good as anyone else's and your

43

algebra and geom. are quite level with mine and Con's. You *are* a goop!"

It was Rosamund's turn to flush. "Oh, Len, are you sure? I'd love it! But everyone seemed to think I'd better dig in at ordinary lessons and miss music ut."

"That was only the first term or so, you ass! You could take it on quite well now. Why don't you let the Gays know?"

"Well, they never said anything and I don't suppose the scholarship covers extras."

Len chuckled. "I shouldn't imagine they ever thought of it. They aren't musical at all. Tom used to say that the only way she knew *God Save the Queen* from any other tune was that you stood up for it and not for the others and no one could expect her to be musical, anyhow, 'cos none of her people were."

"Are you taking any extras at all?" asked a round-faced girl who was enough like Len, though she was very dark and Len was chestnut-headed and grey-eyed, to tell Richenda that here was another of the Maynard triplets.

"I am taking extra art," Richenda said.

"Oh, *poor* you!" This came from two or three people at once.

Richenda stared and forgot her iciness as she asked blankly, "Why on earth?"

"You wait till you've met Herr Laubach," Eve said with a world of meaning in her voice. "You'll know *all* about it then!"

"He has the world's worst temper," Betty added. "If you ask me, he was *born* in a rage and he's gone on being in one ever since."

Len chimed in with a giggle hitched fore and aft of her remark. "When Mamma was at school he chucked her out of his class after first flinging everything at her. They stopped her art lessons after that," she added thoughtfully.

Everyone else giggled, too. Richenda had yet to learn that this was a treasured legend in the school. As it was, she merely felt startled and rather apprehensive.

"But he does make you see what he wants you to do," put

in someone else feelingly. "What's more, unless you're completely hopeless, you do it, more or less."

Primrose Trevoase gave the new girl a wicked glance. "What gets me is the fact that he never speaks anything but German," she said.

"*German*? But I don't know a word of it!" Richenda gasped.

"Oh, you know two, don't you?" Alicia said soothingly "You know that we call supper 'Abendessen'. And breakfast is 'Frühstück'."

"Anyhow, lots of German words sound more or less like English," Rosamund put in. "For instance 'Father' is 'Vater' and 'Mother' is 'Mutter'."

'Ah, but let's hear you *spell* them!" Len said teasingly.

Before Rosamund could do anything about it, Primrose was up again. "No; *you* know now. Let's hear *Richenda* spell them. Go on Richenda! I dare you!"

Richenda gasped again. She had no idea of the vagaries of German spelling. But she could never refuse a dare, so she plunged headlong into it.

"F–a–h–t–e–r," she spelled slowly. "M–o–o–t–e–r. That's how you said them, anyway."

"*Wrong!*" they chorused gleefully.

Con Maynard might be a dreamer, but she was sensitive. She knew that Richenda was feeling annoyed and she didn't think Primrose's teasing very fair. "You *are* a pig, Primrose!" she said quickly. " How could Richenda possibly know when she's never learnt German before? Don't you worry, Richenda! I'll bet you'll soon be making rings round her when it comes to German. She's not so frightfully bright at it herself—*and* she's been learning for ages!"

"Pig yourself!" the discomfited Primrose cried. Then, for she was really a nice girl, she added, "Con's right, all the same. Sorry, Richenda! I was only trying to get a rise out of you. All the same, I'll bet you won't forget either of those two again."

Richenda made no reply and the sound of the gong put an end to the talk; they lined up and marched into the Speisesaal for breakfast. This consisted of bowls of milky coffee, rolls of delicious bread, butter and cherry jam. A good many of the girls—most, in fact—ate these in what Richenda described to herself as "the normal way". But some of them broke up the rolls into the coffee and ate the result with their spoons. Len, who was sitting opposite, saw the new girl's startled face and leaned forward to murmur, "It's all right. That's how they do in Austria and Germany and this part of Switzerland quite often. Mamma told us ages ago."

Bed-making followed Frühstück and Rosamund obligingly showed the new girl the one way in which Matron approved of beds being made. Richenda was accustomed to attending to her own room at the weekends and in the holidays, so she made no demur when she found that she must dust it. She was quick and neat in her work and when Jo, as dormitory prefect, came to inspect, she was able to approve it unreservedly.

They had a walk next with Miss Ferrars as escort, and when they got back they all had to go to Inter V as no one knew yet whether she would be promoted or not, though some of them, like Jo Scott and Len Maynard, were fairly sure of it.

"I hope you'll be with us," Len said to the new girl as she gave her a chair. She had taken a fancy to Richenda despite the very repressive manner that young woman assumed on occasion. "You're in our dormy and you've been with our crowd all the time. I don't say some of the people you've met won't be in Inter V again this year. But if we're moved up to Vb, it would be rather decent if you were there, too!"

"*If* you're moved up?" Prudence Dawbarn said quickly. "You jolly well know *you* are safe enough, Len. You came second with Jo last term. If you two don't go up, who will? Answer me that one!"

"Jo will all right," Len replied. "The thing is they may think we three are too young for it. We aren't fourteen yet and you know how they fuss if they think you are likely to have to overwork. I'm *hoping*, of course, but I'm saying no more."

Richenda remained silent, but she thought hard enough.

She hoped she *would* be in the same form as Rosamund and Len and Jo. She had to own to herself that she was disposed to like them. Of course, she could never be as chummy with anyone here as she had been with Susan. But if she *had* to stay—and she knew that she must—she would have to have *some* friends or be flatly miserable for the next two or three years.

Carmela Walther, who had been listening and who was not shy, struck in. "When shall we know which is our class?" she asked.

"Oh, after Prayers. Miss Dene will read out the form-lists then," Jo said. "And that reminds me! Have you all got your hymn-books ready?"

They all produced them and then Carmela went on with her questions. "How do they decide which class we are in?"

"From your entrance exams, of course," Priscilla said. "You had the papers, didn't you?"

"Oh, yes," Carmela replied.

"Well, then! How did you get on, by the way?"

"Oh, I found some of them easy and one or two very difficult." Carmela spoke fluent English, though with a strong German accent.

"What about you, Richenda?" Rosamund asked.

Richenda, who had spent the whole of a glorious August day sweating over those same papers and had found the French difficult and the German impossible, shook her head. "I could do nothing with the German, of course. I didn't like the French—*nor* the arithmetic. But the English was decent and the history very interesting."

At this point, Miss Ferrars arrived, very official in her gown and B.A. hood, and the chatter had to cease.

Prayers were as impressive as the evening ones had been. Miss Annersley's lovely voice somehow helped one to think of what one was saying and Whom one was addressing and Richenda found herself approving of *this* part of her new school, at any rate.

After Prayers, the Catholics marched in and took their places. When everyone was seated, the Head called on Miss Dene to take register and everyone promptly looked very alert. This was the one day of term on which the school secretary took the roll and a good many people were very anxious to know what their fate was to be. VIa had nothing to worry about. They could go no higher. But it was a question for most of the rest. Richenda, listening with all her ears, waited eagerly when it came to Vb. Luckily her surname began with F, so she was soon put out of her misery. She gave a little gasp of relief as Miss Dene's pleasant voice called, "Richenda Fry!" She answered "Adsum" like the rest and sat back and heard no more. Miss Dene read on quickly until the last name had been called and little Marie Ziegler had piped, "Adsum!" Then she closed the great book and went back to her seat among the mistresses. The Head smiled at her, rose and came to the lectern.

"Now, I have a pleasant task," she said. "First of all, our Head Girl this year is Mary-Lou Trelawney."

The school broke into loud clapping. There was even an attempt at cheering from some of the Middles. Richenda gathered that Mary-Lou was exceedingly popular with all parts of the school. The Head laughed, though she shook her head at the obstreperous Middles before she held up her hand for silence.

"A little less excitement, please! We have a great deal to do and Matron is waiting to unpack you all, so we must go on. Hilary Bennet is Head of the Games. Viola Lucy is Second prefect. The others are Lesley Bethune, Doris Hill, Hilda Jukes, Lesley Malcolm, Meg Whyte, Janet Youll and Josette Russell. Sub-prefects are Barbara Chester, Prunella Davies, Clare Kennedy and Christine Vincent. As soon as they have had their first meeting, you will know what duties each is undertaking. Mary-Lou is also Head of Ste Thérèse's, Hilary of St. Hild's, Prunella of St. Scholastika's and Clare of St. Clare's. These are all the appointments I can give you at the moment. The rest you will find on the notice-boards sooner or later."

She paused a moment and the school relaxed. Then she began again.

"Matron will oversee all unpacking, though your House matrons will be in actual charge of you. When you are

48

dismissed, go straight to your form rooms and wait till someone comes and tells you what to do. A good many of you will have to hand in old textbooks and collect new ones. The new girls have stationery to collect as well. All that must be finished by the end of the morning.

"Now I want to remind you that each day brings its own language. I want you all to try to remember which language you speak on each day and keep to it. It will be a good deal better for your pockets if you do, you know. I *don't* want," her gaze rested reminiscently on one or two people, "to have girls coming to me on Sunday to ask if they may have a little extra for church collections as fines have eaten all their pocket-money away for the week!"

The school laughed appreciatively, but said nothing, and she continued:

"We shall have our usual Christmas play at the end of the term. You will hear more about that later on. Meanwhile, we have to congratulate a number of people who did well in the public exams last term. The lists will be pinned up on the board here and you can study them at your leisure. And now, that is all for the present. School—stand! Turn! Forward—*march*!"

She nodded to Miss Lawrence and now the mistress crashed down on the first chords of that hoary-headed favourite, Blake's *Grand March* and, to its gay tune, the girls marched out and along to the form rooms, Richenda going with the new Vb, and in spite of herself, feeling a thrill at having really attained such a form and so being with the three girls to whom, so far, she was most attracted.

Chapter V

Plans For Richenda

THE new Vb hurried along to their form room. Certain people had been left behind who had been with them in Inter V last year, but were not up to the Vb standard. Among them was the third of the Maynard triplets, Margot. She had given her sisters a very wistful look as they left Hall and Len had bent down and murmured something as she went past.

Arrived with the others, Richenda went to stand beside the wall with the other new girls while the remainder, chattering like a flock of starlings, proceeded to "bag" the desk that pleased their minds. One girl went straight to a window seat and Jo Scott, after a quick glance at her, said, "It's rotten for you, Viv!"

"I know; but if you've been absent the best part of a term with measles and bronchitis on top, it's just what you can expect!" was the melancholy reply. "I missed practically a third of the year's work."

"Oh, well, you'll soon make it up. And it *has* been known for people to be moved up at the end of the Christmas term or even at half term," Jo said.

"Witness Mary-Lou and Co. a couple of years ago!" Vivien said laughing. "Bag your seats, folk. And then we'd better see about desks for the new girls."

Len had already settled herself at a desk somewhere in the middle of the room and Rosamund was next to her. Now the eldest Maynard looked across at Richenda and called her.

"Hi, Richenda! There's room for one of those odd desks over there! Come on, and I'll give you a hand!" She jumped up and went over to where several locker desks, like those already set out, looked as if they were waiting to be placed.

Richenda ran to help her and between them, they moved it to the row where they set it between Len's desk and Rosamund's. Rosamund had moved her own over for the purpose and brought a chair from the pile in another corner. Other girls were busy making the rest of the new girls feel at home. By the time they heard quick, light steps coming

50

along the corridor, everyone was seated and it was to a roomful of very proper pupils that Miss Ferrars arrived.

This broke up almost as the young mistress swung into the room. At least half the form cheered in an undertone and Len cried joyfully, "Oh, are you going to be our form mistress again this year?"

"So it seems!" Miss Ferrars said, looking at them with eyes that were pools of laughter. "What I've done to deserve it, I *don't* know! However, there it is. Now sit down, all of you, and keep quiet for a few minutes if you can."

The girls sat down at once and were quiet and she looked at a small sheaf of notices she held in her hand.

"Well, first of all, Miss Dene wants to see the new girls. Jo Scott, take them to the study, please. Best wait for them too. They won't know their way about yet, of course, and the corridors are something of a labyrinth until you're sure of them. Go with her, you people. Now for the rest of you!"

Richenda and the others heard no more, for they were out in the corridor by this time and Jo was shutting the door behind them. She led them through a positive maze of passages, explaining as they went that originally the building had been a hotel, and the school authorities had built on to it at intervals.

"It makes it a bit of a jigsaw puzzle until you've got your bearings," she said. "However, it comes in time. Through this door—this is the Head's own private wing where her rooms are. The study and Miss Dene's office are here, too, and she and Mlle de Lachennais sleep over here. Along this passage and here we are!" She pulled up beside a door in a narrow passage which was lighted by a long, narrow window looking out across the valley to the mountains at the other side.

Eight girls rather older than themselves were standing waiting, all of them people from Switzerland, France and Germany. Richenda also found that, apart from herself and a roundabout girl with glasses perched on a tip-tilted freckled nose, who answered to the name of Joan Dancey, all new girls in Vb were also continentals.

"We've a lot of foreigners this term," Jo Scott murmured

to her and Joan with an insularity that was superb in the circumstances. "We've always had a few, ever since we came to the Oberland, of course; but this is the first term we've had such a crowd at once. I overheard Mary-Lou and Hilary saying that there were over fifty of them!"

The door opened and a tall, fair-haired girl, obviously German, came out and asked with a marked German accent, "Vich ees Amandine St. Michel? Plees, you veel now enter."

A slightly-built girl with smooth black hair and sparkling black eyes went in at once, and the Va girl in charge of the party called to the other whose name seemed to be Elise Kramer, to come and stand with the rest. Then she glanced at Jo with a twinkling smile.

"Only one more after Amandine and then your crowd can begin," she said.

Jo nodded. "I suppose you came straight here? We had to wait for Ferry. She's our form mistress again this year, did you know? Rather decent for us!"

"Oh, rather! Ferry's a poppet. You folk are in luck."

"Aren't we? Are you a big form this year, Maeve? You seemed larger than usual to me when Dency was reading out the names."

"Twenty-one, my dear! What about you? I thought *your* little lot sounded endless, let me tell you!"

"Twenty-four—so we've got you beat!" Jo retorted. "How are Peggy and Bride? And how's your young Daphne?"

"Quite O.K. As for Daffy, she's a pet! Awfully like Auntie Madge—Oh, hello, Amandine! Finished? Then off you go, Berta. Then we can get back to our form room and begin to do something!"

A rosy, flaxen-haired girl of sixteen or so went into the study to return a few minutes later and announce in German that Miss Dene now wished to see the first of Vb. Maeve gave Jo another of her twinkling smiles and went off with her lambs. Jo opened the door and motioned to Joan Dancey to go in. Joan made a face at Richenda before she took her way into the room. She was out speedily and Jeanne Daudet from Bordeaux followed. Then it was Richenda's turn. She swallowed hard for her mouth had become unaccountably dry. Then she found herself inside a pleasant, book-lined room with flowering plants on the window-sills and a bowl of late roses on the business-like desk before which pretty Miss Dene was awaiting her.

"Come along, Richenda," she said briskly. "I shan't keep you, but there are one or two modifications in your time-table I want to explain to you."

"Yes, thank you," Richenda got out, though why she should have been so scared of Miss Dene was something neither she nor anyone else could have explained.

The secretary felt something odd about her and looked up. "Pull up that chair and sit down here and we'll go over it again."

Richenda did as she was told. Miss Dene produced a great sheet and spread it out on the desk before them. "Now! You have extra art, but not music. Now let me see. Yes; here we are! You go to the studio on Wednesday afternoons from fourteen to sixteen while the others have science which you're not taking."

She glanced up again and caught the stupefied look on Richenda's face. "What's the matter? Oh, *I* know! I forgot you probably didn't realise that here we are in Central Europe and use European time names. We go right round the clock from one to twenty-four, Richenda. Didn't any-one tell you?"

"I—I think someone said something about it," Richenda gasped. "Only—it has such a weird sound and—well I couldn't *think*——"

Miss Dene broke into a peal of laughter. "Oh, your poor face! Never mind; you soon get accustomed to it. Now we must go on. On Monday, Wednesday and Friday evenings, you go to Mlle de Lachennais for extra French and Miss Denny will give you German coaching when she can dodge it in. I ought to explain that this only lasts until you can understand and speak enough to go on with. So the harder you work now, the sooner it'll end. And I'll give you a tip. Try never to go to bed any night without having learned at least five new words of each language. It doesn't take much

53

of your time to rub ten new words into your memory and by the end of the term you'll find you're getting a very good little vocabulary. Of course, you'll pick up a lot by just hearing it all round you. Everyone does. *I* did, in my time. You know I'm an Old Girl, don't you?"

"Yes; Rosamund Lilley said so," Richenda replied, feeling much more at home now.

"Yes; that was when the school was in Tirol. But like you, I came knowing hardly a word of German and not a great deal of French. I was amazed when the end of the first term came and I found I could understand and talk with a fair amount of fluency even in that short time. So will you be. Now is there anything you want to ask before I finish?"

"I don't think so, thank you."

"Good! If anything does crop up at any time, you can always come and ask me between seventeen and half-past and I'll help you if I can. Now, for the last of it. We're putting you in Vb, but if you find you can't manage the work, you'll be moved to Inter V. Don't worry if you find the languages something of a handicap at first. As I've just told you, every day you'll find that part of it growing easier and in any case, we all understand and every allowance will be made for you so long as you don't try to trade on it. But it won't do if you have to work so hard that you upset yourself and make yourself ill. That won't be allowed for a moment. And if we find that you can't keep up, don't think you've disgraced yourself. The thing is that you must do your best in form and during all lesson hours—which includes prep. If, after that, the work is beyond you, then you'll be told and so will the other girls and no one will think or say anything more about it. It's happened before and, I don't doubt, will happen many times again. Now that's all. Good luck to you! Try to remember all I've said and be happy here. That we *do* ask of every girl. Now run along and send Carlotta Kieffen in to me."

She gave Richenda a brilliant smile. That young lady stood up and put the chair back against the wall from which she had taken it.

"Thank you, Miss Dene," she said sedately. "I promise to

do my best." Then she departed, firmly resolved to stay with Vb somehow. Miss Dene might talk as she liked. Being sent down *was* a disgrace and one that Richenda Fry did not mean to endure at any price!

"Carlotta, you're next," Jo said as Richenda appeared, and a very solemn-faced individual went in while Richenda returned to her place among the rest.

"What did she say to you?" Joan Dancey asked eagerly. "*I'm* to have coaching in French and German and maths. What about you?"

"French and German," Richenda said. "She didn't say anything about maths."

"Lucky you! I'm awfully bad at them, but I've done no science or I might have taken that instead. My last school was a little private one, you see, and we didn't go in for things like that. But she said if they found I couldn't keep up with the rest of the form, I'd have to go down to Inter V and I'm jolly well not going to let *that* happen if I can help it!" Joan set her lips and looked as fierce as her cheeky nose would let her.

"Who're you planning to murder!" Jo Scott demanded at this juncture. "Not Deney, I hope! We couldn't spare her! She's what Aunt Joey calls one of the foundation stones— meaning that she was one of the first girls at the school."

"I wasn't thinking of murdering anyone," Joan replied. "Only making up my mind to stay in Vb if I have to swot myself blue in the face."

"You won't be allowed to do that!" Jo retorted. "Overwork firmly forbidden in the Chalet School. We have our lessons and prep and then it's finish so far as work is concerned. So for goodness' *sake*, Joan, don't try to do anything mad like sneaking books upstairs to bed. You'll get caught and have a frantic row and it isn't worth it." She turned away as Carlotta appeared to send the next girl into the study and Joan was left looking rebellious—which was pretty much what Richenda felt. She, too, had been planning to snatch extra half-hours at work and now, it seemed, there would be trouble if she was caught.

"Oh, well, I'll just have to dig in all I can during prep and lessons," she thought. "But I'll show them! I'll show every-one—especially Father!"

It was not a praiseworthy sentiment, but at least it was better than carrying on with her black sulks as she had fully intended to do. But it had struck her already that there wasn't going to be much time for anything like that. You may be able to sulk at home, but when you are at boarding school with a very full programme, it makes it difficult.

She thought all this over while she stood waiting with the rest. Then the contingent from Inter V arrived and the last new girl for Vb came out and Jo marched them back to their form room where they were immediately plunged into the business of getting their text-books from the stock-room. Halfway through that, Matron sent for them to unpack, and when that was over and the text-books had been duly collected, the new girls had to go for stationery. Halfway through came Break with a choice of milk or lemonade and biscuits in the Speisesaal, after which they went out to the garden for a little fresh air. But it was a full and busy morning, all said and done, and by the time the bell rang for the end of morning school the last of Richenda's sulks had vanished. Not, however, her feeling towards her father. She still could not forgive him for making such a clean cut across her life for the very thing that she had inherited from himself.

She remembered what he had said about the Chalet School being a *punishment* for her, and since she was a girl who could reason when she chose, she decided that if she should *enjoy* it, it would put an end to the punishment business.

"And that'll be sucks to him!" she thought.

Chapter VI

A Different Outlook

HAVING most undutifully made up her mind to render her father's punishment null and void by enjoying herself at the new school, Richenda turned her attention to keeping her place in Vb. For the first week, she watched her own work with a concentration that caused Priscilla Dawbarn to label her "a swot of the swottiest kind". By that time, she had decided what were her weakest points and settled down to pulling her work up in those subjects.

Arithmetic was one, of course; but she found that the teaching she got from Miss Wilmot was very different from that under Miss Coulson. What she did not understand was that Nancy Wilmot was a born teacher who loved her work, while Miss Coulson had only taken up teaching because she must do something for a living and that meant good holidays. Even if Miss Coulson had not resigned at the beginning of the summer term, Miss Hilton would have asked her to do so.

Sue Mason wrote a long letter to her old chum, giving her all the news and this piece of information into the bargain. She reported that the new maths mistress was a "stinger" and hoped Richenda had better luck at the Chalet School.

On the second Saturday of term when they wrote their home letters, Richenda scribbled the brief note she was expected to send to her father and then settled down to writing a lengthy epistle to Sue.

"What weird news about Couly! I'm sorry the new one is so ghastly. Here, we have Miss Wilmot, who is a poppet and really does make you see what you are trying to get at. I understand quite a lot already that was a blank to me before and don't swoon, my lamb, but I'm actually beginning to *like* maths! She—Miss Wilmot, I mean—is an Old Girl and frightfully keen on the school. She sometimes goes with us on our walks and she's tremendous fun then. But try to play her up in lessons and you soon know where you get off!

"I like all the mistresses here, so far. Miss Ferrars, our

form mistress is a poppet"—Richenda, like most girls of her age, was given to repetition of epithets—"and everyone likes her. She takes our geography and maths in the Middle forms and Inter V and some English with them as well. Miss Derwent sees to our English and once a week we have a literature lesson with the Head. That's tremendously interesting because you never know what she's going to take. You'd love her, Sue! Do ask your people to send you here!

"Art is pretty fearsome, though I like it. Herr Laubach is an Austrian and frightfully keen and he simply blows you sky high if you don't do exactly what he wants. But he does make you see what it is and why. I've had two lessons with him so far and I can feel I'm going ahead. And I'm getting on in French, too. You know, Sue, when you hear nothing *but* French for a whole day at a time, you just can't help learning things. And here, when they tell you something, you have to repeat it until you say it more or less Frenchily and by the time that happens, you know those words for keeps. You just can't help it.

"The German is the worst of it. I didn't know a word before I came here and I *did* know the usual amount of French. I wish they didn't stick their verbs at the end of sentences. You get accustomed to it in Latin and that's a dead language, anyhow. When it comes to a living one, it's *moithering*! However, I'm beginning to understand some of the things that are said to me, but I'll never get the sort of accent they expect. My throat isn't made that way!

"The best of all is history. Everyone told me that their history mistress had left last term to be married to one of the doctors at the San at the other end of the Görnetz Platz and there would be a new one. And then, when history came along, the door opened and in she walked—Miss o'Ryan, I mean. Only now, she's Madame Courvoisier. The girls just shrieked when they saw her!

"She's awfully pretty—blue eyes, black hair and the loveliest complexion. She's tiny, too, smaller than Miss Ferrars and I can look over *her* head. She grinned when she heard the others and said, 'Yes, I'm teaching you for this

58

term, at any rate. Miss Annersley couldn't get anyone she liked to take my place and I might as well go on with you for the present.'

"Rosamund Lilley—I told you about her in my last—said, 'Are we to call you Madame Courvoisier? I don't think we shall ever remember'. And she said, 'You'll come to it in time. Sure, I got a shock the few times myself when I heard it though I'm accustomed to it now. Do your best and for this half of the term, I'll answer to either. After that, though, you'll be getting no reply from Miss o'Ryan when you speak to her'. We all shrieked.

"By the way, I've got a new name now. I'm Ricki, out of school. Len Maynard began it. On last Sunday she said suddenly, 'Richenda's awfully long for everyday; how do they shorten you at home?' I said I never had been shortened and I didn't see what you could do about it, anyhow. Len said she'd think it over and when we went for a ramble in the afternoon, she and two or three of the others came along, and believe it or not, they discussed it quite seriously. Len said that her real name was Helena and Con's was Constance. They all call Rosamund Lilley, Ros, and nearly everyone with a longish name gets a short. Then she asked how I liked 'Richy' and I said, 'Not at all!' Rosamund said, 'What about 'Shendy' then?' But I didn't like that, either. And then Con gave a squawk and said, 'I've got it—'Ricki' and we'll spell it with an 'i' at the end. It'll look better that way!'

"They'd taken so much trouble over it, I agreed, so I'm 'Ricki' for the future. How do you like it?"

"Finish your letters," said Mary-Lou who was in charge of them this morning. "The bell for Break will be ringing in a moment."

Richenda hurriedly scribbled a final appeal to Sue to beg her parents to send her to the Chalet School as soon as possible and finally signed herself for the first time as "Ricki".

The bell rang just as she finished stamping the envelope and she still had not written to Nanny. However, she could do that next day. She collected the two she had done and handed them in for the mail-box and then went off with the others to claim her milk and biscuits.

There was no going out for them today. They had wakened to find the rain streaming down and everywhere dismally wet.

"The weather's broken," Con Maynard said when they had left the Speisesaal and were in their common room. "Oh, well, it's been a miraculous week. This is the autumn, anyhow. I suppose we couldn't expect it to go on being fine all the time."

"What shall we do?" Richenda asked curiously.

"No idea. Someone will come and tell us presently. Hobbies, perhaps."

"Much more likely to be some sort of indoor games," Rosamund said decidedly. "We don't have the Sale till the summer term now, so there isn't quite the rush to get things ready for it. Who's doing the Evening? I meant to look but forgot."

"It's St. Hild," Len said. "I say, Ricki, Mamma was on the phone to me this morning and she wants us to take you home for tea tomorrow. Will you come?"

Richenda's eyes gleamed. "Oh, I'd love it! Will Miss Annersley let me go?"

"Oh, yes. Mamma always has the new girls to tea during the term. She says as the very first pupil the school ever had, it's her duty. Usually she has people in batches—like last Saturday when she had all Va new girls together. But Cecil, our baby sister, has been cutting teeth this week and she's given everyone a doing. Mamma says she can't cope with more than *one* new girl tomorrow and she's chosen you. She'll have the others next week. Cecil will be all right for a while now."

"I'd love to come. Ought I to go and ask someone, though?"

"Yes, go to the Abbess before Mittagessen and tell her. It'll be O.K."

The bell rang then and they all proceeded to Hall where they sat down and waited to hear what they were to do since no one was going to consider any sort of walk, even in

60

raincoats, sou'westers and wellingtons. They were not left long to wonder. Miss Burnett, the games mistress, arrived and announced dancing in the gym.

This news was greeted with quick clapping. Everyone loved dancing, which meant country and morris dancing on such an occasion. There was a quick rush to the Splasheries when Miss Burnett had dismissed them, to change to plimsolls, and then they all pulled on raincoats and caps and raced across to the big gymnasium, which was in a building by itself with the art rooms, domestic science kitchens and geography room.

For an hour and a half they were kept hard at it, mostly with the more exciting dances, though at intervals they were bidden to sit down while the advanced people showed them more complicated dances. By the time the period was over everyone was breathless and weary, and only too thankful to learn that the afternoon was to be spent in the common rooms reading or playing table games.

In the evening, St. Hild's produced a series of tableaux, the titles of which they had to guess. Most of them were historical, though a few represented well-known pictures. Everyone knew "When did you last see your Father?"; but quite a number were puzzled over the scene where *John Alden* proposes to *Priscilla* on behalf of *Miles Standish*. As for what was ultimately explained to be King Canute ordering the waves to go back, *no* one could be expected to realise, as Miss Wilmot loudly proclaimed, that a mass of green and blue serge curtains humped up by various members of St. Hild's represented the sea! No one guessed it, not even Mme Courvoisier, who had turned up as her husband was at the Sanatorium.

Eventually, the prizes offered for the greatest number of correct guesses were won by Mary-Lou in VIa, Maeve Bettany in Va and Jo Scott in Vb. VIb did so badly all round, that Miss Derwent, the house mistress at St. Hild's, said severely they didn't deserve any prize; however, she relented and it finally went to Clare Kennedy, a girl with a sweet nunlike face which was remarkably misleading, as anyone who knew her could have told you!

61

Sunday was a grey day with no rain, but no sun. Everywhere was floating with water and though they were able to go to church, there was no walk. Further along the shelf the little stream, which was dry in hot weather, was a roaring torrent that threatened to break its banks if the rain came again and no one was taking any risks of a flood. They had the time between church and Mittagessen for finishing their letters or reading quietly.

In the afternoon, most of the girls settled down to reading again. Richenda had not finished her letter to Nanny, so she asked for permission to go to the form room to do so. Vi Lucy who was on duty, nodded, and Richenda went off with pad and pen to seek the peace of the form room. Nanny expected a full account of the week's doings, and Richenda, although she had scribbled hard during the morning period had only finished Friday's and still had the tale of Saturday to add. Some of the girls were talking and she felt she could do better if she were alone. They were not to go to Freudesheim till half-past three, Mrs. Maynard having said that for once, she meant to take a nap in the afternoon. After a series of broken nights, she *needed* it!

Richenda went quietly in her slippers and she had opened the door of Vb and was well into the room before she discovered that someone else had taken refuge here. She heard a broken sob coming from a far corner, looked across and beheld the little French girl, Odette Mercier, sitting at a desk, her head buried in her arms and her shoulders heaving with sobs.

For a moment, Richenda felt inclined to depart as quietly as she had come. Then she closed the door softly behind her, laid her belongings down on the nearest desk and went quietly over to Odette, who was crying so violently that she never knew anyone was there until the English girl laid a hand on the shaking shoulders. Then she looked up with a start. After seeing the miserable face all puffed and swollen with tears, Richenda felt that she must do something about this.

"Odette, what's the matter?" she asked gently. Then, suddenly remembering that Odette's English was practically non-existent, she hurriedly recast her sentence into French.

"Qu'avez-vous, Odette?" she asked.

Odette was much too well away to be able to reply at once. But at last she got it out. "Oh, j'ai mal-au-coeur! Oh, Maman—Maman!" And she sobbed again.

"What is wrong? Is she ill?" Richenda asked, still in her very stilted French—later, she was to wonder how on earth she had managed so well!—"Tell me, Odette, and stop crying so much. You will make yourself ill."

"I wish I could," Odette sobbed. "Then Maman would come to me and I should leave this terrible place and go home again!"

"But—why?" Richenda demanded, startled. "And it is not a terrible place, truly, it is not. Try to stop crying and tell me what is wrong. I may be able to help you."

"No one can," Odette sobbed. "I want Maman and I do not want to stay here."

Richenda stared down at her as she dropped her head on her arms again and cried convulsively. She was at her wits' end to know what to do. She had never had to cope with anything like this before, but cope with it she felt she *must*! The question was—how? She stood patting Odette's shoulder and Odette wept and wept and made no sort of response to all the other girl's coaxing. Finally, Richenda gave it up. She straightened up and looked round the room desperately for some inspiration. She got one!

"Stay where you are, Odette," she said; and left her.

She made her way to the prefects' room and tapped at the door nervously. A voice said, "Come in!" and she went in to find most of the grandees of the school sitting about, reading, doing needlework of various kinds, and otherwise taking their ease. At sight of a girl from Vb, most of them stared. Mary-Lou who had dropped her book, saw the trouble in Richenda's face and rose at once.

"Hello, Richenda! Anything wrong?"

"It's Odette!" Richenda blurted out. "She's crying like mad in our form room and *I* can't do anything with her. Would you come and see if you can help? I expect she can't understand my French. Anyhow, she'll be ill if she goes on."

No one had ever made an appeal of that kind to Mary-Lou in vain. "I'll come," she said briefly. "Where did you say she was?"

"In our form room—Vb. Oh, *would* you, Mary-Lou? I can't do a thing with her!"

All Mary-Lou said was, "Come on!"

Arrived in the form room, she took one glance round. Then she was bending over Odette, speaking to her in the fluent, prettily-accented French which Richenda so admired and envied. This was a very different thing from that young lady's halting remarks and Odette responded to it at once. She lifted her head from her arms, looked up into the sympathetic face, and collapsed into the Head Girl's arms. Mary-Lou spoke soothingly to her and then turned and nodded at Richenda. "Take your things away and go and ask Matey to come here," she said softly. "This is beyond either of us and if she goes on, she'll end by having hysterics. Quickly—Ricki, isn't it?"

Richenda gathered up her pad and pen and fled to seek Matron. It took a little doing, for that beloved Chalet School tyrant was not in her own room nor the staffroom. Eventually, Richenda ran her to earth in the Head's private drawing-room whither, greatly daring, she had finally bent her steps. The girls were not supposed to come to this part of the building unless they were sent and Miss Annersley, entertaining Matron and several other members of the staff, raised her eyebrows when Richenda appeared in reply to her "Entrez!"

"Please, Matron," Richenda said hurriedly, "Odette Mercier is crying herself sick in our form room and Mary-Lou sent me to ask you to come to her."

Matron bounced out of her chair and swept past Richenda almost before the girl had finished speaking. Miss Annersley halted her pupil, who was following.

"One moment, Richenda. Do you know what is wrong with Odette?"

"Richenda shook her head. "No, Miss Annersley. She said she had—had—mal-au-*something* and wanted her mother. I couldn't cope with her, so I went for Mary-Lou and *she* sent me for Matron. She said it was beyond either of us."

"I see. Thank you, dear. Run along, then."

Richenda made her curtsy and sped away to her own quarters. Halfway there, she suddenly pulled up to stand stockstill, and stared at nothing in particular.

"Goodness gracious me!" she exclaimed aloud. "When Odette called it a terrible place I felt quite furious with her! So—what?"

She was unable to answer it, but as she went on her way at a more sedate place, she felt dimly that her outlook had changed.

Chapter VII

Joey Puts Her Oar In

Tea at the Maynards proved all that fancy had pictured. They were met at the door of the tall house by an appropriately tall lady with black hair cut in a straight fringe across broad brows and wound into enormous flat "earphones" at each side of her face. Her eyes were black, too, but although none of the triplets had exactly reproduced her colouring, the four had the same short, sensitive features and Richenda felt she would have known Mrs. Maynard anywhere.

Len, Con and Margot rushed on her and hugged her mightily till she cried for mercy. "You girls are a lot too big for one poor creature to cope with at one fell swoop these days!" she protested laughingly. "And what about manners? Let me speak to Richenda, if you don't mind."

"O.K.—but she's Ricki out of school," Len said cheerfully. "Richenda's such a mouthful!"

Joey Maynard chuckled. "Awfully pretty, though. I must use it some time. You don't mind, do you, Ricki? Welcome to Freudesheim—and welcome to the Chalet School, even if it *is* rather late in the day for that. Come along in and take off your things. Show her where to go, Len. I must get back to the salon. I left the twins and Cecil there and Bruno into the bargain."

"Weren't you *trusting*!" Margot cried, pulling off her raincoat and beret. "Better get back and see he isn't flailing around and knocking things over!"

"Bruno's our St. Bernard," Len explained as she drew Richenda across the hall to a small cloakroom. "Hang up your things, Ricki, and change your shoes and we'll go and see what's happened. Buck up, Con, and don't moon.'

Margot had already gone after her mother and when the other three reached the salon, it was to find her sitting flat on the floor, her mother laughing at her, while a big St. Bernard did his best to wash her face with his wet pink tongue.

"Bruno! Don't!" Margot shrieked, shielding herself as

best she could. "Call him off, someone! He's making an awful mess of my frock!"

But Bruno had looked round and spied new victims, and he left Margot, who got to her feet in short order, while Len dragged Richenda behind a big settee and Con scuttled for refuge to the far side of the playpen, where baby Cecil was rolling and chuckling to herself.

The noise they made between them was deafening, and Mrs. Maynard hastily called Bruno to order. "*Down*, Bruno! *Sit*! That's better! Come out from behind there, you two! Con, stop waltzing round the playpen! You make me dizzy! Margot, you run upstairs and tidy yourself. I'm sorry for such a boisterous welcome, Ricki," she added with a laugh. "Bruno is still quite young and very silly, and he adores the girls, though goodness knows why! That's better! Sit here, Richenda, and I'll present Cecil to you."

She bent over the playpen with a swoop of long arms and brought the baby to plant her down on the apprehensive Richenda's lap. "There she is—our ninth! How d'you like her?"

Richenda, still terrified in case she should drop the precious bundle of chuckles in her arms, looked down at her. "Oh, what a *pet*!" she exclaimed. "What lovely curls! And her eyes! They're even darker than Con's!"

"Ba-booba!" remarked Cecil amiably. Then she stretched out her arms to her mother. "Ma-ma!"

"Can she *talk*?" Richenda exclaimed.

"At eighteen months old? Of course she can! She says 'Ma-ma' and 'Pa-pa' and she tries to say her sisters' names, though I admit her attempts are odd. But she's coming on quickly now. By Christmas, she'll be chattering like a swallow if the rest of you people are anything to go by!" She nodded at her eldest girls and then turned to a corner where two little people were busy with a big box of bricks. "Twins! Come along and speak to Ricki!"

The pair got to their feet and came trotting over and Richenda nearly dropped Cecil in her amazement, for they were as fair as she was dark, with silvery fair locks, big blue eyes, and pink and white faces.

"Felix and Felicity," their mother said. "Rather a contrast, aren't they?"

"Fis-ty!" Cecil remarked and there was a chorus of exclamations.

"Oh, Mamma! She said Felicity!"

"Mamma, she called my name!"

"I say! Isn't she coming on?"

Con stooped over the baby. "Say 'Con', precious!"

"On!" Cecil replied and blew bubbles which made Joey hurriedly rescue her.

"She's dribbling all over the place still! More teeth, I'm afraid." She produced a small towel and mopped up the young lady before putting her back into the pen. "Len, call the Coadjutor. It's time these people went to tea. And Con, you go and bring the trolley in and we'll have ours. Margot, fetch the cake-stand. Papa was in Interlaken yesterday and he brought back a luscious selection for today. Now, Ricki," as the triplets went off to obey their mother's orders, "tell me how you like the school. How are you getting on with the work? It's hard at first having to work in a foreign language, isn't it? But you'll soon have a big enough vocabulary of both French and German to get along comfortably."

"Yes; I feel that," Richenda said. "French, anyhow. Why, only today——" She stopped short and went red.

"Only today—what?" Joey asked with interest.

"Well—something—happened and I just had to talk French and I didn't know I knew so much," Richenda said after a moment or two.

Her hostess nodded. "I know. It happens like that sometimes." Then she let the subject drop, much to the relief of Richenda, and turned to school affairs. There came a tap at the door and a sturdy Swiss girl came to pick up the baby and call the twins to come to their tea in the playroom.

"Thank you, Rösli," Mrs. Maynard said. "Give them their tea and I'll come presently and you can go off. Anna will be back by eighteen o'clock, so you can have the evening. Run along, twins. The girls will pack up your bricks for you and bring them upstairs after tea."

They went off happily and Richenda could hear the high, clear voices chattering away as they went off. Then Con and Margot arrived with tea and Richenda was introduced to a bewildering selection of cakes that were indeed luscious.

"I'm afraid we're hardly a quiet household," Mrs. Maynard said as she poured out second cups all round. "What with twins and a baby and a dog that goes mad on occasion it's too much to expect."

"But you ought to be here when we're *all* at home," Margot put in. "Where's Papa, Mamma? Is he coming back before we have to go?"

"I don't expect so. He's gone off to tea—or rather, Kaffee und Kuchen—with Herr Falke up at the Rösleinalp so I don't suppose he'll be back much before eight."

"Have you heard from the boys?" Len asked. "When you write, you might tell them to write to *us* occasionally. I wrote to Steve last Saturday and he's never even bothered to reply."

"Steve, my lamb, is much too busy. You can see the letters we had during the week if you like. Ricki, have *you* any brothers or sisters?"

"No; I'm the only one. Mother died when I was just a kid," Richenda explained.

The triplets stared at her. This was news to them, for she had said practically nothing about her home life.

"Who chooses your clothes, then? Or do you get them yourself?" Margot asked.

"No, Nanny does that. Oh, I have a say, of course, but she generally picks them out. I did choose most of them to come to school. Nanny said now I was fifteen it was time I began. But it's an awful nuisance."

"I daresay," Joey Maynard said. "All the same, she's quite right. If you don't begin young, you may get the weirdest ideas about clothes and that's good for no one. Have another cake, Richenda? Try one of these nuts-and-honey-and-cream things."

"I couldn't! I couldn't eat another bite!" Richenda said fervently.

"Sure? Very well then. If you three are finished, we'll

69

clear and you can pack up the twins' bricks and take them up to the playroom, Len. Wheel the trolley back to the kitchen, Margot; and Con, put the cakes away. Now, Richenda, I mean Ricki, listen to me. You come to school to learn to stand on your own feet among other things. But if ever the time comes when you feel you need a—a crutch, remember that I'm here. I may be the mother of nine, but I'm still a Chalet School girl and I always will be, even when I'm a great-grandmother doddering about among my great-grandchildren and quavering, "Ah, children aren't what they were in *my* young days!" So you remember! And what are you giggling at?"

"The thought of you as a great-grandmother!" Richenda said as well as she could for her giggles. "I simply can't imagine it! You—you're just like another girl, Mrs. Maynard. Oh, I do think Len and Con and Margot are lucky to have a mother like you!"

Joey Maynard looked at her and then laughed. "I'm not the conventional mother as a rule, I admit. All the same, I can be fierce when I must!"

"I can't imagine it." Richenda suddenly looked up at her. "You—you make me wonder what my own mother would have been like. I don't remember her at all."

The splendid black eyes looking down at her, softened. "That makes it difficult, but I expect she'd have been everything you want in a mother. And you *have* your father, Ricki. Be thankful for that!"

Richenda was betrayed into an indiscretion. "Oh, him!" she said.

Joey gave her a quick look. "Something badly wrong here," she thought. "Oh, well, I can't butt in on her yet. But that sort of thing isn't going on if I can help it. Those two ought to be all the closer because the poor child *hasn't* any mother. The best of Nannies can't make up for that!" Aloud, she said, "You ought to be very proud of him. He's a very well-known man. And here come the girls and I must run upstairs and put Cecil to bed. I shan't be long! Girls, look after Ricki till I come back. Anna will see to the twins when she comes in."

"Shall I go up and look after them?" Len asked. "You know what Felix is!" she added.

"I do, indeed! But I shall be up there myself with Cecil, so no, thank you, sugarpie. You stay and entertain Ricki. You might show her those snaps of the Tiernsee—where the school began, Ricki. We have a holiday house there now and I don't mind owning that I hope the day will come when we all move back again." She waved to them and they heard her running up the stairs like a schoolgirl.

Len had brought an album from one of the low book-shelves which ran round two sides of the room. "Here are the snaps Mamma meant. We spend our summer holidays at the new house, so we can tell you all about it."

As many of the snaps had stories attached, frequently of mishaps and adventures that had happened to Mrs. Maynard, they had not seen half of them by the time that lady's beautiful voice was heard calling them to come up and kiss Cecil goodnight. Len pulled Richenda along with them when she would have held back.

"Of *course* it's you as well! Don't be such as ass! Everyone goes up to kiss the babies good night! Come on and don't keep Mamma waiting!"

Richenda gave in and went with them to hear Cecil chuckle and say "On" and "En" and "Ar-o" which meant her sisters, and then snuggle up to her mother with a satis-fied, "Ma-ma!" Then she was tucked into her cot and they all went downstairs where they finished looking at the snaps and heard more yarns. Finally, they had to say goodnight and fly, for no one had bothered about the time and they had exactly three minutes to pull on their coats and berets and race round by the road, since the garden was still dripping.

"Another time, let's hope we've had some dry weather and you can go by the gardens," Joey Maynard said as she ushered them to the door. "If you're late, Len, tell the Head it's my fault. I forgot all about the time."

"You'd better ring her up and tell yourself before we get there!" Len retorted. "No one loves us if we're late for Abendessen. Come on, everyone!" And she led the flying string of girls down the drive, out of the gate, along the road and, finally into the Splashery where they yanked off their things at the rate of no man's business, for they had heard the gong booming as they raced round the house.

Left to herself, Joey Maynard went to her study and rang up Miss Annersley. "That you, Hilda? Well, please overlook it if the girls are late, will you? I never even thought of the time till Len suddenly yelled that they must go at once."

"How exactly like you!" her friend commented. "Very well, since it's your fault. How are Cecil and the teeth?"

"All right at the moment, but she's still dribbling so I'm looking out for squalls in every sense of the word. I say, Hilda!"

"Well—what? Be quick, Joey! The gong will sound in a minute and whatever happens to the girls it won't look well if *I'm* late!"

"It's just I want to know if you know why Ricki seems to be at odds with her father?"

"Why *who* is at odds with her father? Who are you talking about?" the Head demanded in startled tones.

"Richenda Fry, if you must be proper. Well, go ahead and tell me."

"Trust you to get on to that! Who told you anything about it!"

"She did herself—Oh, not in so many words. What she actually said was, 'Oh, him!' And the scorn in her tone! What's gone wrong!"

"It's too long a story to tell you now. There goes the gong! In two words, then, since I don't want to have you ringing up frantically throughout Abendessen, she disobeyed a strict order of his and not for the first time, it seems. He told me that he hadn't been satisfied with her school for some time and that settled it. She's motherless you know, poor child, and he felt that she was outgrowing her Nanny who has had charge of her ever since Mrs. Fry died—when she was only two or three, I believe. Anyhow, he felt it was high time a change was made. He came to see me when I was in London and asked me to take her. He also let slip the fact that he was going to tell her that this change of schools was a punishment for her disobedience. I felt rather apprehensive about how she would settle down, but so far, everything seems to have gone well."

"H'm! I wonder what she did that was so awful?" Joey mused. "Oh, all right! But I'm getting to the bottom of it sooner or later and so I warn you! It's all wrong for any girl to talk of her father in that tone. And it's worse when they have only each other. I should hate to think of any of my girls behaving like that!"

"Your girls have a reasonable man for a father!" Hilda retorted. "From the little I saw of Professor Fry, I should say he was irritable, unable to make any allowances and without the foggiest notion of how to deal with a girl. I must say I've wished he hadn't made this school business a punishment—the more so since, from what I see of her, it's proving to be *no* punishment at all! Richenda has made friends with your own Len and Rosamund Lilly and one or two more of that crowd, and my own idea is that she's enjoying herself to the top of her bent. So what becomes of the punishment?"

Joey chuckled. "What indeed! Good for Richenda! At the same time, she's fifteen and that's an age which can pick up a grievance and *keep* it! Later on, if no one does anything about it, it's going to make a barrier between those two and that's wrong! Yes; I know I'm the champion butter-in of the school, but I've only done it when I saw it was needed and I certainly think it's needed in this case! Richenda goes home at Christmas looking forward to meeting her father again or I'll know the reason why!"

"I suppose I can't stop you," Miss Annersley said resignedly.

"How right you are! O.K., Hilda. You've told me what I want to know and that's all I need for the present. I'll ring off now and I'll be over as soon as I can to discuss the whole affair with you. Good-bye!"

There was a loud "click!" as she banged the receiver back on its cradle and Miss Annersley laughed and hung up also.

"Well, if she takes Richenda in hand there's no doubt about it that young lady will be turned upside down and inside out and hindside foremost until she does come to her senses! And while I think of it, it might be a very good idea to put her on to Odette, though that is mainly a straightforward case of acute homesickness."

She frowned as she clicked off the light and left the room. Neither she nor, wonderful to state, Matron, had made much impression on Odette who had simply gone on sobbing heartrendingly until Matron had finally packed her off to bed with a dose of her pet soothing mixture which had sent the girl to sleep. That was so much to the good, but, as the Head thought on her way through the corridors, it was something you couldn't go *on* doing. Some other cure must be found or else the school must own itself beaten for once, and Odette sent home.

Chapter VIII

TAKING ODETTE IN HAND

BY the end of a fortnight, Richenda might be very fairly said to have found her feet in her new school. She was quickly growing into friendship with Jo Scott and Rosamund Lilley. She was on matey terms with Betty Landon and her *alter ego*, Alicia Leonard. Primrose Trevoase and Priscilla Dawbarn were also inclined to be chummy. As for Len and Con Maynard, they might be a good year younger than she, but she speedily learned that a year in Canada had given them a much more grown-up outlook than the average English girl of their age. Apart from that, Len, as the eldest in a long family, was very responsible and, in some ways, considerably older than her years. Con was given to dreaming at times. She meant to be a writer when she grew up, and when she became immersed in her brain children she was a hopeless case. Her elders had all learned to dread a certain look in her deep brown eyes. It meant that Con was off in a delightful world which had little or no connection with school and *any*thing might be expected from her!

She had found that if she worked hard and honestly during lessons and prep, she had every chance of staying in Vb. She had plenty of brains if she chose to use them—and here, she did choose. She began to go ahead as she had never done before. Even when the lessons were in French or German, she was able to keep up to a certain extent.

This does not mean that in a short two weeks or so she had ceased to regret the Chinese Room and all its contents. There were times when she had an almost unbearable longing for the glowing colour of the porcelains and the feel of the smooth pastes and glazes; then she was apt to go off by herself and fret. These occasions, however, were becoming rarer, and were shorter when they did come; all the same, she had fully made up her mind that when she left school her profession would be connected with ceramics.

One thing she did like above all else: the amount of time they spent in the open air. Apart from that weekend when she had made the acquaintance of the Maynard household the weather had been glorious, with days of sunshine and fresh breezes. As a result the school spent much of its time out of doors, and Richenda flourished in the clear mountain air.

By this time, as Miss Ferrars could have told you, Vb had split up into little groups and cliques. Richenda, herself, was in the chummery made up of Jo Scott, Rosamund Lilley, the Maynards and that young sinner Primrose Trevoase. Betty Landon seemed to head another composed of most of the wildest members of the form. The three Swiss girls naturally formed their own alliance and Carmela Walther from Bonn was also of their group. Only two seemed to belong nowhere—big Joan Baker who was a long way the eldest in the form, and Odette Mercier.

Odette, after that tremendous weep, settled down into a melancholy which made the staff at large worry over her. Her appetite was poor and, though no one had succeeded in catching her at it, Matron was positive that she cried herself to sleep each night. Her eyes always seemed full of unshed tears and she was pale and getting thin.

Other people besides the mistresses noticed this. Richenda with a feeling that perhaps she ought to give an eye to the French girl, tried to be friendly. She even sacrificed her own wishes far enough to invite Odette to be her partner on walks. But chatter as she might, she never succeeded in winning even the ghost of a smile from Odette—or much more than "Oui" or "Non" in answer to anything she said.

Lately, Len Maynard had been noticing things and she had decided this morning when she saw Odette's mournful face that it was time she did something about it.

The Maynards were Catholics, so they went off to the little Catholic church which served all the villages and hamlets round. Richenda went with the rest to the Protestant church. Services for the school were always held before the main morning services for the other people of the district, so at half-past ten, they were back at school and waiting to hear what the programme was to be.

They soon learned. It had been decided that they might all

take sandwiches and tarts and go off for rambles. They were to be back at school by seventeen o'clock as it grew dark soon now, and up in the mountains there was little or no twilight.

The girls went off in their various forms with mistresses in charge. Mlle de Lachennais, head of the languages, was taking Va down to Interlaken. This left Miss Wilmot their form mistress, free, so she tagged on to Miss Ferrars, who had already invited her great friend Miss Moore, the senior geography mistress, to accompany herself and Vb. The girls were told that they were to go as far as St. Cecilie, a tiny village some six miles or so along the coast road from the Görnetz Platz.

Until they were well away from the Platz, they had to walk in pairs; but once they were beyond the few chalets which gathered round its end, they were allowed to break ranks and they rambled along in groups, all talking as hard as they could go. The day being Sunday, they might use any language they chose and there wasn't a girl in the school who refused to take advantage of that.

Richenda and Len started off with Rosamund and Jo; but before they got very far, those two became involved in a hot argument over hockey. The other pair not being particularly keen, left them to it and went ahead.

"Gorgeous day!" Len said, elevating her small straight nose and snuffing the crisp air rather like a dog smelling liver for his dinner. "I rather wish we could have gone up the mountain. On a clear day like this, there must be a wizard view from the Rösleinalp!"

"I'm quite satisfied with this one, thank you!" Richenda said, waving her hand to the mountains across the valley and nearly hitting her friend in the face. "Oh, look at that lake, Len! How it gleams! Which did you say it was?"

"Thun. That's where we go bathing in the summer."

"I wish we could go now," Richenda said enviously.

"You wouldn't, once you were in!" Len reassured her with a grin.

"Why on earth not? What do you mean?"

"Because the water's too cold, of course. All the lakes in

this part of the world are snow-fed. It's all right in summer when he water gets warmed by the sun. At this time of year, it's icy!"

"Is it?" Richenda asked vaguely. "I say, Len," she went on, "you people all say we have expeditions to different places, but we haven't had any yet."

"Give us a chance!" Len protested. "We've only just begun school this minute—or very nearly that. There hasn't been time to arrange anything."

"Well, when will we?"

"Couldn't say. Half-term, most likely. Where would you like to go?"

"Anywhere! I've never been abroad before. I want to see Geneva and Lucerne and Zurich and—oh, anywhere! There's lots to see, in them, isn't there?"

"Oh, heaps! I say, Ricki, we seem to be miles ahead of the others. We'd best wait a little or Ferry will have lots to say when we meet again. She's a pet, but she has a tongue when she likes!"

Richenda hastily agreed that it *would* be as well to wait a little and they scampered over the rough grass to where a fallen pine tree made a good seat. Len carefully examined both trunk and ground before she sat down or would let Richenda do so.

"It's always as well to make sure there aren't any ants about," she explained. "If they get up your legs, they can give you some nasty nips."

Richenda settled herself comfortably and then turned to see how far off the others were. "Who's that over there walking by herself?" she asked.

Len jumped up and came to look. "It's Odette. What on earth is she doing, wandering round on her own like that? I thought she was with Jeanne Daudet."

"No; Jeanne went off with Joan Dancey and Charmian Spencer. I saw her."

Len looked worried. "I don't like it. We're supposed to keep in pairs, at any rate. There's something wrong with Odette."

Richenda nodded. "She's most deadly homesick, poor

78

kid. I don't see what any of us can do about it, though. I've done my best, but I don't seem to get anywhere with her."

"Well, we'll have to do *something*!" Len said definitely. "If that's what's wrong then she ought to be getting over it by this time. We've been back at school a month now and she ought to be feeling more at home. We can't let that sort of thing go on, you know. The silly kid will end by making herself ill and a nice name that 'ud get the school!"

"I know. I've done what I could. But, of course, my French isn't what you'd call brilliant. That may be one reason."

"Well, we can't let it go on."

"But what can we *do*?" Richenda protested.

"Well, for one thing we can try to make her see how jolly lucky she is to be here. For another, I'll talk to Mamma about her when I see her next. But in the meantime, I'm going to see what *I* can do. You don't mind if I scoot and ask her to join us now, do you, Ricki?" She looked doubtfully at her friend.

Richenda flushed. "Mind? Of course not! We'll both go and then she'll feel that it's both of us wanting her. Perhaps that'll buck her up a little. But you'll have to do most of the talking," she warned. "You know what my French is like and her English just isn't there!"

Len giggled. "O.K. I'll be interpreter. Here! Where does the idiot think she's going? She'll be over the edge if she doesn't look out! Odette! Come *back*! Odette!"

Odette, who had been wandering along without paying much heed to where she was going, started as this reached her, saw that she was perilously near the edge of the steep fall of the mountain, and leapt back like a young goat. The other two sped across the space to come up with her and Len, speaking French, took her arm and gave her a gentle shake.

"What were you thinking about? You might have fallen over the edge! Stay with us now, and don't wander off by yourself. Anyhow, you're as much too far ahead as we are. We must wait for Ferry and the others."

Richenda went round to Odette's other side. "I should have seen that you were alone," she said in careful French. "Stay with us, Odette."

Odette gave them a surprised look and for once her big dark eyes were free of tears. Actually, she had been happy for a moment, dreaming herself back at home again and she had had no idea how near she was to danger until Len and Richenda called to her. She turned to look at the depths from which they had pulled her back and shuddered violently.

"I never saw! I might have been killed! And what would Maman say then?"

"That you'd been ghastly careless, I should think," Len said in her most matter-of-fact tones. "Honestly, Odette, you can't go on dreaming about up here. You must look where you're going."

"*Cave*! Ferry!" Richenda hissed at this point; and the three drew themselves up and looked as proper as in them lay.

Miss Ferrars came up to them looking annoyed. "What were you three thinking of? Len, you at least know the rules. Keep with the rest and don't go galloping on like that or I must make you all croc!"

"I'm sorry," Len said meekly. "We were talking and never noticed."

"It's your business to notice. Don't let me have to speak to you again!"

"No, Miss Ferrars." Len was all that was humbly penitent, but Miss Ferrars had finished with them. She waved them on to join the body of the girls who had gone past while she was scolding, and went to join her own friends.

The three followed after the others, Len remarking, "Well, it might have been worse. How everyone would have hated us if she had really made us croc!" She repeated this in French for Odette's benefit and then added briskly, "and now we're going to talk to you in English—slowly. Then you'll understand. You ought to be steaming ahead now. Ricki's doing it in French."

"I—I do not understand. Who is Ricki?" Odette stammered.

"Me," Richenda said with a broad grin. "Len says my name's too long, so she's pitched on that for a short. There's one thing, Len. You can't shorten Odette!"

"We might call her 'O'," Len suggested with a giggle.

Odette stared. "But that is not a name at all," she said.

"Shorts usually aren't," Len told her cheerfully. "Now you try to talk English. And I'll tell you what!" with a sudden inspiration. "We'll talk French and you talk English and we can correct each other. It'll help us no end!"

"*You* don't need any help in French," Richenda said. "You talk as well as Odette does. But I'll be awfully grateful if you *will* help me, Odette."

She spoke very slowly and clearly, and since Odette had managed to pick up *some* English during the four weeks, she understood. "But I would *like* to help you, Richenda—but no; you say Ricki. You have been kind to me."

Richenda went scarlet. "What rot! I haven't done a thing—oh, how do you say it in French? What's the French for 'what rot', someone?"

"'Quelle blague!'—at least I think that's near enough," Len said. "Go on, Ricki! This is a jolly old chance for you!"

Thus encouraged, Richenda did her best and in a moment or two, Odette had become sufficiently interested to join Len in correcting both grammar and pronunciation.

Miss Ferrars had been watching them with a queer expression on her face. Miss Wilmot finished a diatribe on the shortcomings of Francie Wilford's maths and caught it. "What's eating you, Kathie?" she demanded.

"That!" said her friend nodding across at the trio. "Isn't it just like Len Maynard? And she seems to have dragged Richenda into it as well."

Miss Wilmot looked across to where all three were talking vigorously and, where Odette was concerned, with much waving of hands. "Oh! Ye-es! I see! But you know, Kathie, Len is very much her mother's girl—more so than any of them."

A sudden peal of laughter from Len was echoed by a feeble one from Odette and the mistresses gasped.

"Well!" Miss Moore exclaimed. "Len actually seems to be doing something about that wet blanket of a girl! I've known some homesick folk in my time, but Odette could give the whole lot spades and aces and beat them hands down!"

81

"What's Odette's background?" Miss Wilmot inquired.

"Only child of a widowed mother who had kept her close at hand ever since she was born. The father was killed when Odette was a baby of a few weeks old and, from all I can gather, there are only very distant relatives," Miss Ferrars said.

"What about previous education? Or did Maman teach her into the bargain?"

"She had a governess. Her home is a beautiful old chateau at least ten miles from anywhere—Joey Maynard got all this from Simone de Bersac, by the way, and handed it on to me in case it was useful. I'm very sorry for that child, Nancy. She rarely had any chance to mix with other girls and she and her mother seem to have been all in all to each other."

"Then how on earth did the good lady stiffen her upper lip enough to send her away off here?" Nancy Wilmot demanded.

"Simone de Bersac! The governess had to go home because her stepmother died suddenly and the father was left with half-a-dozen youngsters on his hands. Simone happened to be visiting her at the time—Mme Mercier, I mean—and Simone says she leapt at the chance and advised that Odette should be sent here along with her own Tessa. I believe she had an awful time doing it, but she got Mme Mercier to agree at last. It's rather important that Odette should settle down and be happy, otherwise I don't know what's going to happen to her later on."

The other two looked at her with startled faces. "Do you mean—is anything wrong with Mme Mercier?" Miss Moore asked.

Kathie Ferrars nodded. "She's got a rocky heart. She may live for years—or she may go at any time. Simone told Joey that it's the main reason why she went on and on at Mme Mercier until she got her to agree."

Nancy Wilmot nodded. "You know," she said with seeming irrelevance, "it's no wonder that most of our girls grow up helping each other all through."

"What are you getting at?" Miss Moore asked in startled tones.

"Oh, Rosalind! Use your wits—if you've got any! Haven't we all had the steady example of our Old Girls to bring us to it? When I was at St. Scholastika's—my first school, I mean; not the house here—no one bothered overmuch about that. As soon as we joined up with the Chalet School which happened when I was about fifteen, I felt the difference. It's a settled tradition. And, with any luck, it's going to mean that that poor girl Odette isn't going to be left without friends or relatives, even if her mother dies."

"She certainly isn't now Len Maynard is on the job," Kathie Ferrars agreed.

"Yes, and I should leave it to Len," Miss Moore said decidedly. She began to laugh. "Goodness knows how they're managing with language difficulties! I admit Len is equally fluent in either, but Richenda's French is still greatly to seek and Odette has a very poor pennyworth of English!"

"Oh, they're probably using that lovely *lingua franca* we've all used in our youth," Nancy Wilmot said. "Either that, or Len is working double tides, doing interpreter. I should watch Odette, Kathie, but otherwise leave it to Len—and Richenda. They'll manage better than *we* can."

Chapter IX

THUNDER IN THE OFFING

By the time they had reached St. Cecilie, Odette was looking distinctly happier and, between this and the fresh mountain air, even had a little more colour in her face. The new girls looked eagerly round the place. There were about a dozen chalets and farmhouses with a tiny whitewashed church with the usual onion-bulb spire at one end. They had to cross a plank bridge over a little stream to reach the village itself and the girls noted with interest that, thanks to the fine weather they had been having, it was a mere trickle at present.

"But," Len said, "I've seen it simply hurtling along when we've had anything like rain or after the thaws."

"Is Cecil just Cecil or is her real name Cecilie?" Richenda asked.

"Marya Cecilia. She's called after our nun aunt," Len explained.

"Who is Cecil?" Odette asked shyly.

"My baby sister. You'll see her when you come to our place to tea, Odette."

"I've never heard you talk of an Aunt Marya Cecilia," Richenda said.

"No, but you've heard us all talk of Auntie Rob," Len returned. "She's always been called Robin because, Mamma says, when she was little, she was round and jolly just like a robin. She's at La Sagesse in Montreal and she teaches. Some day when we've enough cash for it, we'll all go to Canada again to see her. I'd love to see Canada again!"

"You have visited la Canade?" Odette asked.

Len nodded. "Years ago when we three were just small kids. Margot had two years of it. She went the year before we did with our Auntie Madge and then we went the next year."

"Now then, you three, stop mooning!" said Miss Wilmot's voice behind them. "Len, you and Con run along to the Prieswerk farm and ask for our milk, will you? You

84

wo know more patois than anyone else and Frau Prieswerk speaks little else. Here's the money—and here's Con coming along. Hop off!"

"Can Ricki and Odette come with us?" Len inquired.

"Can *who* and Odette?"

"I mean Richenda." Len had gone very red.

Miss Wilmot laughed. "So *that's* how you abbreviate it? Yes, take them by all means. There should be two cans, so they may help you carry them. Mind you don't swing them too violently. We want milk, not semi-butter!"

"It couldn't be butter as soon as that," Con said seriously, "but we might waste a lot with splashing. We'll be awfully careful."

"Well, mind you are!" Miss Wilmot turned away and they set off across the sweet, thymey turf for the farm where Len's tap at the door was answered by a big, sonsy woman whose olive skin and snapping black eyes told of southern ancestry.

"Guten tag, mein Mädchen!" she greeted Len. "Was ist es, hein?"

Len laughed and explained in her best patois, whereat Frau Prieswerk nodded and went off into a flood of what Richenda mentally called "gibberish". She certainly knew not a single word that was spoken, though Len and Con replied when they could get in a word edgeways. At last Frau Prieswerk went off to seek the milk after ushering the quartette into a room of the kind neither Odette nor Richenda had ever seen before. There were two casement windows with a narrow bench fixed to the wall beneath them and a long well-scrubbed table stood before the bench. At one side of the room was a green-tiled stove with wide shelves to sit on round it. There were two or three of the peasant chairs they had in the Speisesaal at school, and another bench was fixed to the wall opposite the stove. On the wall beside the windows, hung a cuckoo clock and there was a shelf above them on which stood some fine specimens of peasant pottery. The floor was bare of carpet or rug, but it was painted a light maize colour and looked as if it were scrubbed every day.

"I should think you could really eat your dinner off this floor," Richenda remarked to Len. "Why don't they have mats or something, though? It looks awfully bare, just the wood floor!"

"I don't know. I never thought about it, somehow."

"We can ask Mamma. She probably knows," Con added.

"And there aren't any curtains at the windows either," Richenda pursued. "It must be awfully draughty in the winter! And what do they do at night?"

"Close the shutters, of course," Len said, pointing to the shutters which were laid back against the wall outside. "Hang out and you'll see."

Thus, when Frau Prieswerk returned with the two big cans of milk, it was to find her guests hanging out of the windows, admiring the shutters. She set down the cans with a hearty laugh that brought them back into the room in a hurry, all flushed and embarassed. But she waved aside Len's stumbling explanation that Richenda and Odette had never been in a Swiss house before.

Len paid for the milk, called Odette to help her with one can and left the other for her sister and Richenda to bring along. Richenda eyed Con rather doubtfully. She had become quite friendly with Len during the early weeks of the term, but so far as she was concerned, the second Maynard girl remained something of a dark horse. She was friendly enough with most folk, but unlike both Len and Margot, she had no special friend of her own. Con had spent part of her summer holidays in struggling with a play in blank verse. That had been shelved for the moment, but as everyone knew, when the fit seized her, Con was lost to the world, living in a delightful one of her own with the result that the other girls frequently felt that she was withdrawn from them.

Since the beginning of term, Con had been concentrating on her school work. She was by no means as clever as either of the other two and had only reached Vb by a scrape. She was finding that if she meant to stay there, she must keep a firm grip on her poetry, and so far, she had succeeded. Today, however, lines had begun to sing in her brain, and, as

Len had remarked earlier in the day in some consternation, "Con has that half-asleep look of hers coming on!"

Richenda had had no idea what Len was driving at, but she could see for herself that only a part of Con was attending to her. She wondered what on earth it meant. However, she decided to ignore it and start up a conversation.

"What *was* that queer language you talked to Frau What's-her-name?" she queried.

"Patois," Con returned, half-dreamily. "All the country folk in Switzerland used to talk it at one time I believe."

"But don't they now?" Richenda was keenly interested. "Is it only in the mountains that they use it?"

"No; all over the country, of course." Con was rousing up. Richenda's tone had been sharper than usual and had penetrated her consciousness. "It's different in every canton—in some ways. The French and Italian cantons speak Romanshe and the German ones speak Schwyzerdutch which is a kind of German."

"How frightfully odd!".

"Oh, I don't know. After all, you get a Yorkshire farmer and—and a Cornish farmer together and I'll bet if they used their own dialects neither would understand more than half the other was saying. And then *we* haven't been overrun over and over again by other countries as the Swiss have—at least not for ages now."

"Yes, I suppose that *would* make a difference," Ricki agreed. "When was the last time?"

"During the Napoleonic Wars. The French marched in and the Swiss had a ghastly time with them. Then they had to chuck it and at the Treaty of Vienna, every country agreed that in future, Switzerland should be neutral. If you've noticed, even old Hitler didn't do anything about them and it would have been awfully easy for him. He'd only to send an army across Lake Constance. All the north shore of that is Germany, you know." Con had forgotten her poetry in the interest of this.

"Is it? I didn't know. But Con, how did you three learn it?"

"Oh, picked it up. This is our fourth year here, you

know. It's easy if you know Latin. There's quite a lot of Latin in Romanshe. Mamma says that if you know that, you don't have much difficulty with Italian or Spanish or any of those languages because they're all derived from it—even Roumanian. D'you like Latin, Richenda? I do myself. But I loathe and abominate maths!"

"Oh, so do I!" Richenda said fervently. "Thank goodness, I'll never need them when I get to the job stage!"

Con turned deep brown eyes alight with interest on her. "Oh? You've decided already, then? What are you going to do?"

"I'm going to keep a gallery," Richenda said calmly.

Poetry gave a last gasp and died for the time being. "A *gallery*? What *do* you mean? What *sort* of a gallery? Pictures and statues and things like that?"

"Well, I suppose they might come into it; I hadn't thought about them. What I really mean is a gallery of porcelains, and specialise in Chinese porcelains."

"I should think that would be rather fun! But where will you get your china?"

"Buy it, of course, as cheaply as I can. Then, when people come to my gallery to buy, I'll charge more than I paid for it and make a profit."

"But—but I thought people went to galleries to *look* at things—not to buy."

"You sell and buy in the kind of gallery I mean," Richenda said decidedly.

"Oh?" Then mischief flashed into Con's face and she added, "but you *will* need maths for that—arithmetic, at any rate. What about bills?"

"Yes, I'll need arithmetic. But I shan't need either algebra or geom., thank goodness! I can't see why I have to learn them when I shan't need them and loathe them so much— even with Willy!"

"Yes, Willy's a poppet, isn't she? But *I* asked Papa that and he said, 'To teach you to reason, my child'. How'll you start out on a thing like that, Ricki?"

"Oh, I expect I'd have to be apprenticed to one of the big people to learn the trade. It'll mean going right into it from the beginning—serving in a shop, you know, and learning about prices and how to handle customers. And I'll have to swot up all about pastes and glazes——"

"Now then, you two! Where do you think you're going?" demanded Miss Moore as she caught them up as they went wandering along without any heed to where the rest were awaiting them. "We want our milk, thank you! If you *don't* mind, I think you'd better come along and join us. You can continue this conversation in your next! Come along, and stop dreaming, both of you!"

Both went red, but they made no reply nor did she wait for one. With a hand on Richenda's free arm, she steered them over to where the party was squatting about on fallen logs or doubled-up raincoats laid on the ground.

Coffee and milk filled the plastic mugs the girls carried in their knapsacks and then everyone set to work on her package of food. A meat pie, sandwiches, a fruit pie and a slice of cake all went where they would do most good, and were followed by fruit.

"I feel better!" Rosamund remarked to Len as she wiped out her mug with a paper napkin before returning both to her knapsack. "Oh, I was hungry!"

"So was I!" Len said with heartfelt earnestness. "But then, I mostly am at meal times. Papa says we're better to keep a week than a fortnight!"

"Yes, but Mamma says it's because we're growing so fast," Con put in with a chuckle. "She said that she hoped when we'd got through this stage, we'd have more ladylike appetites. At present, we eat more like bears than girls."

"That," said Len reminiscently, "was the day we finished a loaf and a half for tea. But the boys were there, too."

Richenda giggled. "You *must* have appetites! What fun it must be to have brothers! I often wish *I* had one! It's lonely at times when you're an only child."

"But what is that?" Odette asked in her own language.

"It means what it says. You haven't brothers or sisters," Len told her.

"Ah, like me, then," Odette replied.

"Yes—and Ricki, too. I should hate it myself. We often

fight among ourselves, but never about things that really matter. And the boys may rag us, but we rag back."

"How still it's gone!" Rosamund said suddenly. She looked round uneasily. "The breeze has fallen. Look! There isn't even a leaf moving!"

"Oh, it's just the wind gone. Probably it's changing quarter," Betty said easily. "The sun's quite bright, still, and the sky's blue."

Weatherwise Len shook her head. "More likely a storm's coming along," she said.

"A storm! With *that* sun and sky! You're crackers!" Betty protested.

"Oh, no, I'm not! I know the sun's still shining, but it's a queer shine. I'll bet you what you like that if we could see over the mountains, we'd see the sky as black as ink towards the north!" Len spoke positively. "There's a storm coming all right. Ought we to tell Ferry or someone?"

But there was no need for anyone to tell any of the mistresses. The queer stillness had struck them at almost the same moment as it had struck Rosamund. Miss Moore had jumped up and was racing over the grass to the edge of the shelf where she turned and surveyed the north. A moment later, she was tearing back at full speed.

"Pack up and be quick, everyone of you!" she cried. "Len, you and Richenda take those cans back to the farm and *run* for all you're worth! Raincoats and berets, everyone! Now look sharp! There's a storm coming up and we don't want to be caught so far from school if it can be helped. *Quickly!*"

They got down to it in short order. Whatever the new girls might think, the old hands knew well enough what a bad storm might mean at this time of year, and while Len and Richenda dashed off to the farm with the empty milk cans clattering and jingling, the rest swooped down on the raincoats and wriggled into them, tucked all oddments into their knapsacks and slung them over their shoulders, pulled on their berets and then waited anxiously until the other pair came tearing back. "Lines, please!" Miss Ferrars called. "Quick! There isn't a moment to waste and we mustn't be storm-stayed or it may mean an all-night affair. Now *run!*"

Chapter X

RACING THE STORM

MISS WILMOT tore up to the head of the line, crying as she went, "'Ome, James, and don't spare the 'osses!" which had the effect of relieving the fears of some of the more nervy people. Miss Moore took the middle station and Miss Ferrars, being nominally in charge of the party, remained in the rear to act as whipper-in to any laggards.

The girls set off, running at a steady pace. Once they were off the grass and on the coach road, it wasn't too bad. They ran in grim silence. The sun was still shining, but even the most ignorant of them saw that it was with a queer, uncanny light, and ahead they could see that the blue of the sky was dimming. Clearly, the storm was well on its way.

They were six miles from home, but the mistresses hoped that they would have covered at least part of that before the rain came. There was always the chance that if the wind rose again, it might drive the clouds in another direction. They could not hope to escape the rain altogether, but the worst of it might not reach them.

But the most active schoolgirl cannot run for very long distances, and before long it was plain to be seen that there were bellows to mend among the weakest members of the party. Neither Alicia Leonard nor Charmian Spencer was very strong and Charmian was at school because her eldest brother was at the big Sanatorium at the end of the Platz for observation. The mistresses watched the girls carefully and when they had covered the first mile, Miss Wilmot slowed to a trot and made the leaders do likewise.

"No use wearing us all out in the first few minutes," she observed.

But now there came the first faint, long rumble of thunder. It was far away still, but it was quite unmistakeable. Then they turned a curve in the road and the north lay open before them. A violent storm was in progress there and it was travelling towards them and travelling fast. Miss Wilmot jerked out a firm, "Keep on trotting!" to Emerence Hope and Priscilla Dawbarn who were leading, and then fell back to confer with her colleagues.

"We can't make it!" she gasped. "The girls are tiring and they won't have got their second wind before that's on us! What shall we do?"

"There's that big barn about half-a-mile further on, isn't there?" Miss Moore was panting, but her mind was working clearly. "Best make for that!"

"And pray that it won't last all night!" Miss Ferrars added, not ceasing to keep her eye on her charges. "Joan—Joan Baker! Keep up! Don't lag!"

Joan Baker, who was terrified of thunderstorms, gave a little cry and forced her weary legs to keep up the trot.

"I wish—we'd asked the folk—at St. Cecilie's—to put us—up!" Miss Ferrars choked out.

"Too late for that now! And they couldn't have done it—not room enough!" Miss Moore panted. "I know exactly where the barn is. Shall I take the lead?"

"Go ahead!" Kathie Ferrars said no more, and Miss Moore shot ahead, and catching at Emerence Hope's hand, shouted, "We'll shelter in the barn further along! Come on, girls! We've got to make it or be soaked through! *Run!*"

At that moment, a jagged flash of lightning tore across the grey clouds that were boiling up on the horizon. A crash of thunder followed after an interval that seemed endless to the girls. Miss Moore nodded.

"We can make the barn if we keep going!" she told the other two, shouting to make herself heard above another peal. "It's still pretty far away. But it's coming up fast. Keep going, girls! We'll be all right!"

Most of them were very tired now and were beginning to stumble. Then Odette tripped and if Len and Richenda had not caught her, she would have fallen headlong.

"They can't do it!" Miss Ferrars spoke in a strained voice. "They'll have to walk. Some of them are almost done. Tell them, Nancy."

"*No!*" Miss Wilmot exploded. "Let those who can still run go ahead. The rest must walk and I'll keep with them. You two go on with runners."

92

They obeyed her without question, Miss Moore calling to those who could, to run with her and Miss Ferrars and the rest to keep with Miss Wilmot, who had already slowed to a steady walk. Then she raced ahead with Emerence and Priscilla, hoping to reach the barn in time to wrench the doors open for the rest to get in quickly. She suddenly remembered that the hay harvest would be in and wondered how much room there would be. Oh, well, they must manage as best they could.

Kathie Ferrars was also wondering—wondering if they would reach the place only to find it locked. If they were unable to get in, then they must just shelter as well as they could at the sides, and she had little hope that that would be much use. Perhaps one of the big motor ambulances from the San. would come along and they would be able to pack in the weaker members of the party like Odette and Charmian and Alicia. She knew it wasn't likely, but it might just happen.

They turned another curve and the north was hidden again. But among the pine trees which grew in thick black ranks down the mountain slopes, she could see the tall, spire-like rod that crowned the barn and which, for the first time, she realised was a lightning conductor. They would be up to it in a minute more. She was thankful for apart from her anxiety for the girls, she was nearly out of breath herself and a cruel stitch was taking the remainder of her strength. They had a final burst and then Miss Moore dived among the trees and headed for the tiny clearing where the barn stood. Another minute and she and those girls who were still able to do it were tugging at the great doors and finally got one open.

"In you go!" she said grimly to those nearest. "It's pretty full, but you can pack along the sides. Let's hope the rain keeps off until the rest get here."

"Where's Len?" Con demanded agitatedly. "I thought she and Ricki would be here by this time."

"They're helping Odette. Go on in!" Jo Scott said firmly.

"I'll wait here till I see them," Con returned with equal firmness. Then she gave a cry as a blue streak zigzagged across the path, to be followed almost at once by the worst crash they had had so far. It drowned Con's words, but her action was reply enough for Jo, who ignored her, stepping aside and pushing the next girl safely home.

Meanwhile, Nancy Wilmot, considerably more alarmed than she appeared, was doing her best to keep the weaklings on the move. She had Charmian and Alicia on either arm and was herding Rosamund and Joan Baker, Len and Richenda and Odette, Jeanne Daudet and Vivien Allen well in front of her. Running was beyond them now, and most of them stumbled as they walked; but she kept them at it relentlessly. It seemed an endless trudge before they reached the path among the trees, but they did it at last and she called out to hearten them, "Here we are! The barn's straight ahead! Just anoth——" She was left stunned with the word unfinished for at that moment, the lightning struck violently between them and the barn and there was a fearful clap of thunder which seemed to go on and on unendingly.

Holding her breath for fear of damage to either the girls or the nearby trees, the mistress stood rooted to the ground. But mercifully, the lightning had struck into the earth. The turf was scorched black, but no other harm was done. Nancy Wilmot made a final effort.

"Into the barn, all of you! RUN!" she bawled. And, roused by her terrific effort from the stupor into which the shock had sent them, the girls suddenly found breath and strength to tear up the path as if wolves were at their heels. They all reached the barn safely, just as the black clouds swept across the sky and the light was shut out with a suddenness that made them all exclaim.

"Shut that door!" Miss Moore commanded. "The barn won't take any harm, but if the door's left open, there's no saying what might happen to the hay."

Miss Wilmot pulled the door close and then dropped down against the side of the haystack, gasping for breath and mopping her face with her handkerchief. The girls all followed her example. Most of them were finished and all felt they couldn't have gone another dozen yards, even if the rain were pouring down wholesale. There was silence for a moment. Then the thunder pealed again, long and loud. Len Maynard, who had been joined by her triplet and was sitting in a heap with her, Richenda and Odette, sat up, pulled out her handkerchief and mopped her face.

"Oh, my goodness! I'm boiling! You all right, Odette? Sit up properly between Ricki and me. That's better. It's a bit stuffy in here, isn't it?"

"I wish it would rain!" Con said nervously. "I never mind a thunderstorm if it rains, but I do loathe it when it's just thunder and lightning and *no* rain!"

The rain came at that moment crashing with a steady drumming on the roof of the barn that made any talk impossible. The thunder pealed furiously at the same time and everyone was nearly deafened.

They sat in silence, clutching each other's hands. Miss Ferrars was recovering from her stitch and trying to make herself heard above the noise as she shouted to know if everyone was safe and unhurt. A crash of another kind drowned what she was saying and a voice muttered in her ear, "Oh, my gosh and goodness! That's a tree struck! Let's hope it hasn't fallen across the doors of the barn or how on earth are we to get out when this is over?"

She recognised Jo Scott's voice and replied, turning her head in its direction, "We shouldn't have to stay here long. I imagine the farmer will come to make sure that nothing's happened to the barn."

A strangled yelp replied. Jo had had no idea it was her form mistress to whom she was speaking and the shock rendered her nearly speechless.

Meanwhile, Nancy Wilmot was giving Betty Landon an equal shock, for when that insouciant young lady, with no idea who was next to her, demanded in clarion tones, "D'you suppose the stream will have overflowed? And shall we have to *wade* across?" she replied cheerfully. "Well, Betty, you never know. But you can all take off your shoes and stockings to do it! I, for one, won't face Matron if I let you arrive back with shoes and stockings soaked with paddling!"

Betty gasped and sat back, completely silenced for once. Miss Wilmot chuckled to herself. Then she suddenly sat erect—and nearly upset Priscilla Dawbarn who had been leaning against her with no real idea who it was.

"Miss Moore—Miss Ferrars!" she yelled. "That peal wasn't so loūd! I believe——" What more she would have said was lost as the thunder pealed again. But the people near enough to have heard her also sat up, for they recognised the truth of her statement. The storm was travelling rapidly and the thunder was certainly not quite so loud. But it left the rain behind it. When, greatly daring, Miss Moore contrived to open the door a few inches, she found it pitch dark and the rain coming down in torrents. The thunder might be passing, but they certainly could not go out in that!

"And the worst of it is," said Len to no one in particular, "that thunder sometimes rolls round and round the lakes for hours on end. It may come back again. Goodness only knows *how* long we'll be stuck here!"

Richenda whistled. "That so? What will they think at school?"

"Oh, they'll expect we found shelter somewhere," Len said easily.

Kathie Ferrars was fully recovered. "Well, we seem to be settled here for the present," she said. "What about having a singsong? Strike up, girls! *Drink to me Only!* We all know that!"

She began it, but pitched it too high and they found themselves squeaking on the top notes. Joan Baker made no attempt to get them. She suddenly dropped to the octave lower and then found that she had to growl on her bottom notes! The effect was too funny for words and the girls stopped singing and burst into peals of laughter, after which, everyone felt better. Miss Moore had been investigating and now she called, "There's enough coffee left to give everyone a tiny drink. Fish out your cups and I'll come round—if I *can*!—and share it out."

It *was* just a tiny drink, but it made them feel better again and when it had gone, Len, who had been keeping an eye on the crack between the doors, gave a sudden shriek. "Oh, Miss Ferrars! I believe it's getting lighter! Look! You can see quite a little! Perhaps the rain will calm down and we can get home."

The mistresses—indeed, everyone—looked eagerly and saw that she was quite right. The light was beginning to grow. The blackness was turning grey and though all they could see was a curtain of steadily falling rain, it was much better than seeing nothing. Miss Moore opened the door further and presently they were sitting in a twilight which brightened every moment though the thunder was still to be heard in the distance. Then Jo Scott cried that the rain seemed to be easing off and the moment it was possible to see through it, the mistresses acted. They had no wish to spend the night in a barn! Neither did they want to await a return of the thunder so far from home. Everyone was hustled out, raincoat buttoned up to the neck and beret pulled well down over her eyes.

They were to have one more adventure before they reached the safety of the school. They made good time along the road which was glistening in the grey light of the rainy skies, but quite possible to negotiate. They covered a mile easily and were well on the second one when a squall from Emerence and Priscilla halted them. "What's wrong?" Miss Ferrars cried, running to the head of the column.

She stopped dead when she got there. The trickle over which they had passed on the outward journey had swelled to a torrent which had broken its banks and what Richenda called "A young lake" had spread across the road and the grass and was lapping the stems of the trees further back. They might be able to wade so far, but, as Miss Moore, eyeing the pouring torrent sagaciously, observed, in the middle the force would be tremendous—quite enough to take some of the lighter girls off their feet.

Nancy Wilmot nodded. "There's only one thing to do— and mercifully, we aren't likely to have any spectators but ourselves. I'm the biggest of the party, so I'll tuck up my skirts, make for the bridge—the handrail is a good foot above the water—and see if it's possible to wade across that way.

Both Miss Ferrars and Miss Moore protested, but she gave them a calm smile.

"Then what do you propose to do? March the girls back to the barn for the night? Or do you prefer to hang about here, waiting for that ghastly storm to strike again?"

They had nothing better to propose, so she pulled off her shoes and stockings, rolled up her skirts to her waist and set off, feeling every inch of the way with her friend's stout stick. She made it, though she gave them one sickening moment when she seemed to stagger on the bridge. But she was gripping the handrail and steadied herself just in time. Then she was back again, wringing wet from the knees downwards, and none too dry otherwise.

"I think we can do it. The bigger ones must each be responsible for a smaller one and they must cling together and never take their hands off the rails until they have to. Luckily, they go quite a way outside the banks at each end. Come on, Jo! I'll take you first. Once you're past the stream itself, you can finish your own paddling. Off with your shoes and stockings everyone, and tuck up your clothes as I did. Once we're over, it won't take us long to get home!"

Hand in hand with Jo, she waded out and when they reached the bridge, the girls saw the pair with inside arms locked and outside hands gripping the rails firmly. Miss Moore and Miss Ferrars watched them with their hearts in their mouths. Three minutes later, Jo was wading on alone and Miss Wilmot was coming back.

Joan Baker might be afraid of thunder, but water held no fears for her. "Shall I go now and take Rosamund, Miss Ferrars?" she asked. "I'm the biggest of us girls. I can come back too like Miss Wilmot."

Before anyone could reply, Miss Wilmot was calling to Con Maynard and setting off with her and Joan, clutching Rosamund by the arm, was following. This set the other girls off. Betty took Alicia who went very quakingly for she *was* afraid. But they reached the far side in safety, and by this time quite a number of the girls were well over.

Len turned to Odette. "Your turn next, Odette. Don't be afraid. Here's Betty coming for you and she won't let you slip. Cling to the handrail and you'll be all right." Then Joan arrived for herself, and Miss Wilmot who was looking very tired now, came for Richenda.

That young lady opened her eyes when they reached the bridge. She had never felt anything like the force of the water. It took her all her time to keep on her feet, even with Miss Wilmot's arm firmly round her and her free hand clutching the rail. But at last she felt the pull slacken, and then Miss Wilmot left her to go the remainder of the way herself while she went back to fetch her colleagues who had insisted on waiting until the last girl was over. Miss Wilmot stood five foot nine and was plump and sturdy; but Miss Moore was slender and as for Miss Ferrars, she was a small woman and would have stood no chance against the fury of the stream.

At long last, they all stood on the farther side. They were wet and cold, but home seemed much nearer now and a minute later, their troubles ended. As they trudged along, the sound of engines was heard and then two convertibles appeared, one driven by Dr. Maynard and the other by his friend and colleague, Dr. Graves. They drew up as they saw the long line of wet and weary girls approaching them through the rain which still fell steadily. They asked no questions, but they piled the adventurers in, getting everyone squeezed into place somehow. Then they turned cautiously and less than ten minutes later, the convertibles pulled up outside the school where a bevy of anxious people awaited them.

No one asked any questions then. Dr. Maynard bundled them all out and handed them over to the body of matrons with instructions that everyone was to go straight into a hot bath and then bed.

The baths were ready for them and by the time trays were brought round with coffee, rolls and butter and cakes the girls were all safely in bed with hot water bottles to comfort them, and most of them so tired that it was hard work to keep awake. The doctor arrived and swiftly examined everyone. Finally, in "Matey's" room, he gave his verdict.

"I don't believe they'll even catch colds. Leave them to sleep it off. Give them each a dose of that patent nostrum of yours, Matey, before they go off, though. I'll be in in the morning to make sure and we may have to keep two or three in bed for the day to get over it completely. But I doubt if we have any real trouble."

"And thank God for that!" said Miss Annersley who had been with Kathie Ferrars and got a more or less full account for all their adventures. "But it'll be a long time before I let them go off on a Sunday ramble again!"

Chapter XI

THE STAFF AT LEISURE

"IT was an adventure," Nancy Wilmot said meditatively. "No one can deny *that*!"

"An adventure I could have very well done without!" Kathie Ferrars retorted. "I never thought, when I applied for a post here, that I was going to live through such hair-raising experiences! The very first term, I was nearly thrown down a crevasse in a glacier and I was stiff and sore for ages after. The next term, we had a fire——"

"*We* didn't," Miss Derwent murmured. "That was at the Hall by the San."

"We were in it though!" Kathie returned severely. "I admit last term was fairly quiet, but that was mainly owing to the coming-of-age celebrations. Now, this term, we've had *this*! I only wonder my hair isn't white! I never felt anything like the force of that water when we were crossing the bridge. When I thought that I had allowed some of the girls to come and go through it over and over again, I felt sick—and still do when I think of it!"

Nancy gave her a quick look. "Kathie, you goop! The responsibility of that part of it was mine and not yours. And do you really think I'd have agreed if I hadn't known that the girls could manage all right? There's a difference in weight between a shrimp like you and a hefty young thing like Joan Baker or Betty Landon. And now, that's enough about it! What I want to know at the moment, is what everyone is doing at half-term. Which of us are on duty, for a start? Rosalie! Is it fixed up yet?"

Miss Dene glanced up from the jigaw puzzle over which she had been bending for the last half hour. "What's that you were saying, Nancy? Oh, half-term! I've got the duty list somewhere on me. The Abbess and I were doing it after Kaffee und Kuchen and I think we've got it all settled. Now where is it?"

She fumbled in the pockets of her cardigan and finally produced a folded sheet of paper which she spread out. "I meant to take a few minutes this evening to type it for the noticeboard in the staffroom, but I saw this thing on the table and sat down to it instead."

"Fatal!" observed Miss Armitage, the science mistress. "Once you sit down to a jigsaw, you've had it! I remember once sitting up till two in the morning to finish one. Well, now you've been recalled to your duty, tell us the worst and let's get it over. Who's on the free list for a start?"

Rosalie Dene smiled sweetly at her. "Oh, no, you don't. You'll take the thing in proper order or wait till tomorrow morning to hear the news. Take your choice!"

"Brute!" Miss Armitage exclaimed. "Very well, we're in your hands. Get on with it, do!"

"Well, first of all, all the girls are going off by forms as usual—except for the Maynards and Richenda Fry."

"I suppose Joey wants her trio at home for her own reasons," Kathie said. "But why not Richenda, may I ask?"

"Father's command," Miss Dene returned briefly.

"Father's command? Rosalie, what *do* you mean?"

"Just what I say. Father, it appears, sent Richenda to school here as a punishment for deliberate disobedience—"

"Which is a complete washout. Young Richenda is enjoying herself to the top of her bent," Nancy Wilmot interrupted with a rich chuckle.

"Exactly! Though he knows nothing about that so far. But it seems that at the time, he also informed her that she was to stay at school for half-term. He wasn't having her back home, first, because it was too expensive and second, because she was not to see the place before Christmas, by which time, he hoped she'd have learned the error of her ways and go back prepared to obey on the moment. No one can blame him for the first. It *would* be much too far and much too expensive. But when I think of the second, I wish I had a good heavy object in my hand and the chance of clonking him over the head with it!"

"How fierce!" Nancy exclaimed. "You *are* worked up over it!"

"He makes me *feel* fierce! He seems to have no idea that staff have any claims to consideration whatsoever. You

102

know what happens. We send circulars round to all parents or guardians, stating what is going to happen and asking them to confirm consent. We got his notice and back came a very stiff letter. He regretted upsetting our plans, but Richenda was to have no treats at all this term. She was obstinate, disobedient and undeserving of them. She was to stay at school and he hoped that her mistresses would set her work to do over the weekend which would keep her well occupied!"

Shrieks from the others interrupted her. She waited until they had finished their recriminations and then she went on.

"The Abbess then sent him a personal letter, explaining that there would be no mistresses on duty as they would all be away, and requesting him to reconsider his decision. Back came an even stickier reply. He imagined that at least some of the domestic staff would remain and if she was given plenty of work, he expected they could see to her. In any case, he refused to bear the expenses of the trip."

"*Well*! I do call that cool!" Kathie exclaimed. "Anyhow, as this is the long half-term of the year, there won't be even Karen left in charge—not from Friday night till Monday night, anyhow. So what happens then?"

"Joey happened in just as the Abbess was reading this and was called in consultation on the spot. She came to the rescue at once, of course."

"But of course!" murmured Mlle de Lachennais, leaving the coffee-pot to look after itself and coming to join the agitated party. "She will be at home herself, n'est-ce-pas? As she is having her own girls at home, we may take that as understood."

"Quite right, Jeanne. She insists that Richenda joins them. The fact of the matter is that some business concerned with the San has cropped up and Jack has to go for consultations with Jem Russell and the rest of the Board. He'll be away three weeks at least, so Joey decided to go with him, taking the twins and Cecil. In the circumstances, Joey decided to have the girls at home for the weekend. She wailed long and loudly about the whole affair. She's in the middle of a new school story and she hasn't a hope of getting it finished before they go, so she'll be late with it for once.

She got monotonous after a while, so I chipped in with a suggestion that she might be able to help us over Richenda. The Abbess instantly backed me up and we told her the whole yarn. When she heard it, she demanded Richenda as makeweight. And if Professor Fry's ears weren't nearly scorched off his head by the time she had finished giving us her unvarnished opinion of him, they ought to have been! She let herself really go and coined several new epithets on the spot with which to describe him!" Rosalie suddenly stopped and went off into shrieks of laughter at the memory. "The Abbess's face when she really got going! I nearly wept with laughter!"

"Tell us what she called him!" Nancy Wilmot pleaded.

"I couldn't remember half of them. One thing was 'a rumbustious crocodile'. Even the Abbess giggled over that!"

"I don't blame her!" Ruth Derwent declared as well as she could for her wild mirth. "I wish I'd been a fly on the wall to get the whole beauty of it!"

"Well, the upshot of it all was that Richenda was instantly booked and I had to write a very stilted letter to him explaining that the whole place would be closed from Friday till Tuesday so Richenda couldn't possibly remain; but the mother of three of our girls whose home was up here had offered to have her and we had made arrangements accordingly. His reply came this morning. He isn't at all pleased about it, I may say, but he can't do anything but agree. Even a furious father could hardly insist that a girl of fifteen should be left alone for four or five days in a huge, rambling place like this! But he still hopes that she will be given plenty of work to do and that we'll explain to Mrs. Maynard that she is to have no treats of any kind. She is to be made to toe the line!"

Kathie Ferrars sat up, wiping the tears of mirth from her eyes. "And what did Joey say to that one?" she inquired with interest.

"Said she should use her own judgment and if he didn't like it, he could do the other thing! To judge by the look in her eye; I should think Richenda will *not* find the weekend entirely treatless!" Rosalie wound up with a chuckle.

"I shouldn't think she would," Nancy Wilmot agreed. "But does the kid know anything about Father's kind ideas for her half-term?"

"Not from us," Rosalie said firmly. "I can't say, of course, what he may have written to *her*."

"Let's hope he manages to hold his tongue—or his pen—on the subject!" Ruth Derwent went on. "Does he *want* the girl to hate him?"

"No; I don't think that. The Abbess thinks that he really has her good at heart. But he's going quite the wrong way with a proud, sensitive girl like Richenda."

"What exactly did she do that's worked him up so?" Miss Armitage asked.

"Interfered with his beloved porcelains, I believe, after she'd been forbidden to touch them. I'm not really very sure. However, she goes to Freudesheim and how she spends her half-term will be Joey's affair. For no one is going to set her any work. The girls all work hard enough during lessons hour and they need the break as much as we do."

"Quite so," Nancy replied. "And now that we've had all that, would you mind answering the original question and telling us what the rest of us are to do?"

Rosalie turned to her list. "The two sixths are going to Freiburg in charge of you, Davida," she said, turning to Miss Armitage. "Miss Denny is coming with you."

"Good!" Miss Armitage was clearly very pleased. "I'm very fond of Sally Denny and though the sixths are quite good companions, there are times and seasons when you want an adult to discuss things with you."

Rosalie nodded and went on with her lists. "Nancy, you take the two senior fifths, and Peggy Burnett will go with you. You're going to the Valais with headquarters at Sion which is supposed to be one of the loveliest cities in the country."

"Can do," Miss Wilmot said contentedly. "It'll be new ground to me as well as the girls." Then she sat up with a bounce. "Len Maynard's going to have something to say about this! She told me last term that she did wish we could have an expedition to the Valais as she was dying to see the Matterhorn."

"Len can go any time. She lives here," Rosalie reminded her. "Anyhow, Jo wants them, so that will be that. Dorothy," she looked at the head of the music staff, "I have to break it to you that you have Inter V—but *not* Prudence Dawbarn, Primrose Trevoase or Francie Wilford. Those three and Priscilla Dawbarn are going to Paris. Mr. Dawbarn will be there on business for his firm, so Mrs. is coming with him, and they asked for the twins and said they might each bring a friend. I hope they realise what they're doing, inviting two scaramouches like Primrose and Francie along with their own pair of demons!"

"Thank goodness!" Peggy Burnett said fervently. "With those four beauties out of the way, both you and I, Dorothy, may hope for a fairly peaceful half-term."

"Oh, Primrose and Priscilla are getting a little more sense," Kathie said, firing up at once on defence of her own form. "Primrose is really no more trouble than anyone else, whatever she may have been."

"Well, you *do* surprise me!" Peggy Burnett said with a grin. "I remember that the first term she came, her father begged the Abbess to provide herself with a cane and *use* it!"

"Oh, never mind that!" little Miss Andrews exclaimed. Do go on, Rosalie, and tell the rest of us what we have to do! Where are my babies going, for one thing?"

"Your babies, my child, are going to Montreux—but you won't be with them. Joan Bertram has them and her own form. You're free this half-term. So you'd better be thinking out what you want to do."

"Who else is free?" Mlle inquired.

"You for one, my dear. And Frau Mieders for another." She leaned back in her chair to call across the room to Frau Mieders, the domestic science mistress, who was knitting quietly in a corner. "Hear that, Anna?"

"I did. Thank you, Rosalie. I shall to Kufstein go to see the little Gretchen and my mother," Frau Mieders said placidly, not ceasing to knit.

"Kathie, you're free, too, and so is Biddy o'Ryan, of course. By the way, everyone, Biddy is really leaving us at the end of this term. She came to the office this morning to tell me. We must see about some presents."

"Leaving? Not really?" Kathie's voice was sharp with disappointment. "I hoped she'd stay on till the end of the summer term, anyhow."

"My dear girl, by that time, Biddy's hands will be very full. Anyhow, we all knew that any further stay of hers at school, once she was married, would be a very temporary affair. We've been lucky to keep her so long. But don't look so upset, Kathie. Biddy may be busy, but she'll have plenty of time for her friends, just as Joey has."

"It's to be hoped she doesn't inspire Joey to start in again," Nancy Wilmot said. "Nine's quite a family in these days and quite enough for one woman."

"No one can say what Joey will do next and I, for one, won't prophesy. But Biddy is very thrilled and looking forward eagerly to May. She told me she hoped for twins, but she'll be satisfied with whatever comes along. Now let me finish or the rest of you will have to wait until the morning, by which time I hope to have got this thing typed out and pinned on the board."

"You won't do either now!" Nancy Wilmot said, rising to her feet as the bell rang for Prayers. There's the bell and we must go. This room's in a pretty fair mess. Some of us must come and tidy up afterwards. I will, for one. Who'll come with me?"

"I will!" came from Kathie Ferrars, Ruth Derwent and Davida Armitage.

Peggy Burnett shook her head. "I've got a list of things I want Matey to get when she goes down to Interlaken tomorrow, and I've never touched it yet. I must get down to it after Prayers so as to give it to her before we go to bed. But I'll do it tomorrow if you three will see to it tonight—and that's a promise."

"Good! Then come on! It won't do for staff to be late! Bad example to the girls!" And Ruth Derwent, laughing as she went, headed the long line of ladies who proceeded decorously from their sitting-room into the corridor and down the front stairs to part in the entrance hall, some going to Hall and the rest to the gym where the girls were already assembled and waiting.

Chapter XII

THE PROFESSOR UPSETS THINGS

THE notices about half-term were on the noticeboards in both the staffroom and Hall by the next morning, and the school buzzed with excitement.

"The Valais!" Len Maynard shouted exultantly. "Oh, miraculous—marvellous—*spiffing*! It's the one place I *did* want to go to! I'm yearning to see the Matterhorn and Monte Rosa, and besides I'd love to see the vineyards!"

And then the Head sent for her and her sisters and informed them that they were not going with the rest as their mother wanted them at home this half-term.

Len's face fell almost comically. "Not go with the others? Oh, Auntie Hilda!"

"But *why*?" Margot, the youngest of the three, demanded succinctly.

"You don't listen, Margot. I told you your mother wants you."

"But why does she want us just *that* weekend?" Con asked wistfully. "It isn't that we don't love to go home and see her. But we've wanted to visit the Valais for ages and we were thrilled to the back teeth when we heard that our form was going there."

"She and your father have to go to England for three weeks or so shortly after, and she wants to see all she can of you girls while she's here."

The three were silent and eyed each other thoughtfully. Miss Annersley quaked at what might be coming. She was in Joey's confidence, as no one else was, and she knew that there was just a chance this this young lady might be away from home for a good deal longer than six weeks. But the girls were not to know yet. For the past months or so, she had been having attacks of pain and sickness. Jack Maynard, always on the alert where his precious wife was concerned, insisted that she must go to London for a complete overhaul by an old friend, Sir James Talbot. This business of his provided a very adequate excuse for her being away, and would keep the girls from worrying until news of one kind or another *must* be told to them.

Margot was the first to speak. "But she does see quite a lot of us, anyhow. What's the idea of having us at home for *half-term* weekend? It—it'll spoil all our fun. I don't understand. It's not like Mother!"

Miss Annersley looked at her thoughtfully. "I don't see that. Aren't you being selfish, Margot?"

She left it at that and Margot went red and said no more. Len looked at her brevet aunt with eyes that were full of suspicion. "What's behind it all, Auntie Hilda? Margot's right, you know. Mamma wouldn't do a thing like that just because she was going to be away for two or three weeks. She was down in Montreux for six weeks or so when she went to take over Aunt Winifred's house while she had appendicitis. But that didn't make her bag our half-term. What does it mean?"

"Is the three weeks just a blind, and is she going for longer than that really?" Con demanded.

Poor Miss Annersley! She had guessed that the trio would be likely to probe deeply, and she did not know what to say. "She said that your father must go on business and he would be away for three weeks at least," she began. "She wants to see your aunts and all the babies, and it's a good opportunity. She's taking the twins and Cecil with her and Freudesheim will be closed for a fortnight to give Anna and Rösli a good holiday. Besides, do you never think that parents may sometimes be glad to get a rest away from all such responsibilities as you three? You wouldn't like it if we expected you to go on at school all the year round; but you seem to expect to have your father and mother at your beck and call all the time. In any case, that's what has been arranged, and you must make the best of it!" she finished tartly, carrying the war into the enemy's camp.

The triplets had no more to say, but Len looked very dissatisfied. In some ways, she was older than her sisters, even that young sophisticate, Margot. She felt that there was something behind all this that was being kept from them and she wanted to know what it was. Miss Annersley knew what she was feeling, but she had no intention of saying any more. She dismissed the other two with the remark that they had better go and think what they could do to enjoy their weekend. Len she kept back for a minute or two. Con and Margot departed, casting on their sister looks which said that if she, as the eldest, was to hear anything further, they expected her to tell them about it at the first opportunity. The Head knew this, but she ignored it, and the pair curtsied and went out. When they had gone, she turned to Len who was standing looking at her with grave grey eyes.

"Len," she said, "I have some news especially for you. Richenda Fry is coming with you to Freudesheim for the weekend."

Len knew a certain amount about Richenda's home troubles by this time, and the gravity left her eyes as she said eagerly, "Has her father said she's not to go with the others? She was rather afraid he might."

"What do you mean?" Miss Annersley said.

"She told me that she was in an awful row with him when she left home. I think it's still going on, and from what she's told me, it's the sort of thing he might do. Is that it, Auntie Hilda?"

Miss Annersley made up her mind swiftly. "I'm afraid it is, Len. But you are to keep it to yourself—unless Richenda herself says anything more to you."

Len looked hurt. "I don't babble! *I'm* not a leaky cistern!"

"Where on earth did you pick up *that* expression?" gasped the stunned Head.

"I read it somewhere and I thought it hit the nail awfully well. It's not slang, is it?"

"No, it's not slang. As a matter of fact, it comes from the Bible—I can't tell you exactly where at this moment so don't ask—but it's not a phrase I like. I'd rather you didn't use it again."

"O.K.," Len said easily, for the "Head" had gone and it was "Auntie Hilda" who was talking now. "Well, I'm awfully glad Ricki is coming to us if she can't go to the Valais. But I must say I think that dad of hers is the outside of enough!"

"I don't suppose your opinion of him would worry him in the least!" "Auntie Hilda" told her crushingly. "I don't want to hear it either."

Len grinned. "I don't suppose I'll ever get the chance to tell him, and, of course, I quite see that you've got to stand by another grown-up. Auntie Hilda, does Ricki know that she's coming with us and not to the Valais?"

"Not yet. I want you to send her to me now so that I *can* tell her. So suppose we close this conversation, and you go and find her. Off you go!"

"All right. And may I tell Con and Margot that she's coming?"

"Not until I've seen her. Then you may, but she must know first."

Len departed, nearly forgetting her regulation curtsy when she reached the door. She bobbed it hurriedly at the last moment and then went scuttering through the corridor to change into plimsolls and pull on her blazer before racing off to seek her friend on the netball courts, where she guessed she would be practising, as this was free time for them.

Richenda was hard at work, shooting at one of the practice goals. She had taken to netball like a duck to water, and was very anxious to play in the form team. She had a straight eye and a level head, and as Miss Burnett had once remarked, showed signs of becoming an excellent shooter. As her friend reached her, she was throwing from a tricky angle and Len held her breath as the ball circled the rim of the net before condescending to drop through neatly.

She clapped vigorously, and then as Richenda turned to her, startled, she said, "Oh, *jolly* good, Ricki! You're coming on like hot cakes! That was a really nasty shot! But I say, the Head wants to see you."

Richenda picked up the ball and turned to her. "What's that? I mean," as she suddenly remembered that this was Tuesday and a "French" day, "Qu'est-ce-que-c'est?"

"Madame désire ta présence dans l'étudier," Len said, dropping easily into French.

"Oh goodness!" Richenda lapsed dismally into English at this. "What have I being doing now?"

"Que tu as de mauvaise conscience!" Len giggled. "On l'en dit lorsqu'elle te recontres. Dépêches-toi!"

"Pas de tout! Ma conscience est toute en éclair," retorted Richenda struggling with her vocabulary and grammar, and making rather startling mistakes in both. "Je ne peux pas— er—*remember* quelquechose que j'ai fait du tort."

"I'll put that into decent French for you later," Len said cheerfully. "I can't now. The Head is waiting for you." Then she added, "Hand over that ball and I'll have a go at shooting myself. Come straight back and tell me. I'll be here."

"That depends—er—cela dépends combien longue elle me détaint," Richenda returned, capping her previous mistakes with this final remark.

Len giggled, advised her to tidy herself before she went to the study, and set to work to practise shooting. Richenda raced off, first to the Splashery where she splashed her face and hands and ran a comb through her rough curls. Then, satisfied that she looked fairly respectable, she set off for the study. She tapped at the door and then entered, remembering to make her curtsy before she went up to the desk. Miss Annersley gave her a smile.

"Come along, Richenda. Take this chair. Now, dear, I know that your father told you that you were not going home for half-term. I expect you know by this time that very few of the girls do. Switzerland is too far for it to be worthwhile for such a short time."

"Yes, I see that," Richenda said, completely at her ease since this could not mean that she was to be called to account for any forgotten sin. "It's all right, Miss Annersley. I knew I wasn't going, and I'd rather go to the Valais, anyhow."

"But you aren't going," the Head said quietly. "Neither is——"

What else she was going to say was drowned in the sharp cry Richenda gave. "Not going? But why? It can't be my work! I was sixth in form last fortnight and I've been simply slogging to get fifth this time!" Then her face suddenly changed, growing sullen. "Oh, I suppose it's some of his great idea about punishing me! It's just the sort of thing he *would* do!"

112

Miss Annersley still spoke quietly, though there was sternness in her voice as she said, "That is not the way to speak of your father, Richenda. Also, I must ask you not to interrupt me so rudely." Then she relented as she met the miserable eyes. "If you had waited, you silly girl, you would have heard that the Maynards aren't going either. Mrs. Maynard wants them at home this weekend as she and Dr. Jack are going away for a few weeks on the tenth. She has invited you to go with them to have a taste of home life with them."

Richenda flushed and wriggled uneasily. "I'm sorry I interrupted you, Miss Annersley. I didn't mean to be rude," she murmured unevenly.

"Then we'll say no more about it. You'll have a very good time at Freudesheim if I know anything of Mrs. Maynard. And you and Len are great friends, aren't you? I don't think you'd have enjoyed even the Valais quite so much without her, would you?"

Richenda stared at her, wide-eyed. Like most school-girls, she had no idea that the Head kept close enough tabs on any of them to know about their special friendships and it came as a shock to her to learn it. She remained silent and the Head pushed her advantage home.

"You've never had the fun of living in a big family, I know. The boys won't be there, of course. They are all at school in England. But you'll have Len, Con and Margot, and there are the three babies as well. I expect Mrs. Maynard will let you help her bath Cecil. Have you ever had anything to do with a baby?"

"No, nothing. Do you think she would? I'd love that!" Richenda eagerly.

"I'm sure she will. And she'll certainly have various kinds of fun arranged for you people. You'll have a very good time, you'll find."

Richenda's face had cleared and she gave her Head a wide smile as she said, "It sounds simply terrific! Do Len and the other two know?"

"Len does; I told her to say nothing to her sisters until I had told you. But you may tell them about it now. That's all

113

I wanted you for, so you may run along. Find the Dawbarns and send them to me, will you? Thank you, dear!"

Richenda went off to seek out Len and plunge into delighted chatter with all three Maynards about the half-term prospect. She was so excited that she nearly forgot all about the Dawbarns. Luckily for her, she met Priscilla as she was tearing off to the netball court, and stopped long enough to give her Miss Annersley's message before she shot off again to find the triplets practising passing, though they stopped as soon as they saw her. Con and Len were frankly delighted and Margot liked Richenda well enough to be quite pleased about it, though she did murmur something about wishing Mother had asked Emmy, too. But Emerence Hope was another not going on the Valais expedition as her parents were in Geneva, and expecting her to join them there.

For the rest of the week, Richenda was happy. She worked hard and her marks were so good that she even ventured to hope for fourth place on the form lists—bracketed with some of the others, of course! But Tuesday before half-term brought a change. The Professor had *not* restrained himself and in his weekly letter he told his daughter plainly what his plans for her were.

"I understand that the school will be closed for the weekend, so you cannot remain there. Your Head Mistress tells me that the mother of another of the girls has offered to take you. I hope she will see to it that you work during the weekend. I have written to Miss Annersley asking her to speak to the mistresses who teach you, and request them to set you enough homework to keep you busy most of the time. I shall expect to hear that you have done all they give you and done it well. Please understand that until your behaviour shows that you deserve to have treats, you will not have them. So far, I have seen little sign of that."

The truth was that he was bitterly hurt by the very brief and stilted letters that she wrote him—mainly because she *must*—each week. He took them as a sign that she was still quite unrepentant. Somehow, he was determined to make her toe the line and he tried to do it by severity. The result was that the wall building between them grew quickly. It was a real pain to him, for they had only each other, and to judge by her letters, Richenda didn't care whether he was there or not.

What made things worse was the fact that he knew that she wrote volumes to Nanny, and only the week before, Mrs. Mason had met him and told him that from the long screeds she sent Sue at wider intervals, Richenda was enjoying herself thoroughly and making real strides in her lessons. As enjoyment had *not* been his idea when he sent her away, he resented it.

Richenda didn't understand, either. To her mind, he only wanted to make her as miserable as he could. She contrasted his attitude with all she had heard from the Maynard girls who seemed to adore their father; and Rosamund and Jo and one or two others, and she made up her stubborn young mind that he didn't care about her at all. If he did, he wouldn't be so beastly to her!

As a result, she went off into her old, brooding behaviour. For two days, she was thoroughly miserable. No one had *said* anything to her about lessons for half-term, and she knew that no one else would be expected to work. But it was just like him and she *hated* him!

It was Miss Ferrars who interfered in this promising state of affairs. She saw with consternation that Richenda's work was falling off badly and she couldn't account for it. Nothing had happened in school to cause it or she would have heard all about it. One morning, when Richenda was late in putting away her things, the young mistress came into the form room in search of some papers she had forgotten. They were alone, and Kathie Ferrars seeing the unhappy look on the girl's face, decided to find out what was wrong.

"Oh, Richenda!" she said. "The very person I want to see!"

"Now it's coming! She's going to set me that beastly homework!" Richenda thought, and she looked, if possible, more sulky than ever as she waited.

"I want to know what's gone wrong with you?" Miss Ferrars said, coming to perch on the lid of a nearby desk. "Aren't you well? Have you got toothache?"

Richenda stared at her. "I—I'm quite well," she stammered, forgetting her manners in her surprise.

"Then what's the matter? Can't you tell me? Perhaps I could help to make things straight again."

Richenda remained tongue-tied. Kathie Ferrars bent forward, her own vivid smile flashing over her face. "Come on, Richenda! It can't be anything very bad!"

Richenda found her tongue. "I don't know what *you* call very bad," she said in choked tones and quite forgetting that she was speaking to a mistress, " but how would *you* like to be told that you were to have prep to do all the half-term holiday?"

"Oh, *drat* that man!" Miss Ferrars thought, most reprehensibly. Aloud, she said, "Oh no, my child! That you are not! Apart from the fact that no one has any time either to set you prep now or correct it after the holiday, no one in this school is allowed to work during half-term—not even exam people. If you people are to work properly during the term, you need the break. No one can go on working at full pitch all the time. And that reminds me, *your* work has gone off very badly this last few days. If this is what's been doing it, you can snap out of it at once. You'll get no prep from me nor from anyone else, so far as I know. Now run along and don't be so silly! Half-term is half-term here, and *no* one works!"

Richenda had nothing to say. Miss Ferrars' breezy treatment rendered her speechless and almost breathless. Kathie Ferrars chuckled to herself as she picked up her papers and sauntered out with a nod to the girl. But when Richenda finally recovered herself enough to shove everything into her desk and dash off to the Splashery to tidy herself before Mittagessen, the sulky look had vanished. There was no need for her to have been so wretched all this time and she needn't have let her work go to pieces as she had done. For the three days that remained of the half-term, she would slog as she had never slogged before and retrieve her position somehow.

With this in mind, she went ahead as she had never done in her life, and when on Thursday afternoon the form lists were read out, she found that if she had not reached her coveted place, at least she was still sixth, and considering the marks she had lost earlier in the week, that was amazing.

"And I only wish I could write home and tell him it's sucks to him and his grand idea of spoiling my half-term!" she thought. "I can't. He'd probably take me away from here and I *don't want to go*. But I'm just not going to bother about him any more that's that!"

Chapter XIII

JOEY

"WELL, that's the last of them till Tuesday evening!" Len Maynard turned to her sisters and Richenda with a broad grin. "Come on, folks! We'd best trot over home now. No point in standing around here and we can't get in anywhere. Besides, Mamma will be waiting for us and I rather *think*,"— this very pensively—"that she's got some miraculous ideas bout half-term fun."

Con picked up her cello case and went with Margot who was burdened with her viola. Len had a fiddle. As Joey Maynard had once said, "My family seem to have taken a hate at the piano. Felicity will *have* to take it on, though, or there'll be no one to play accompaniments!"

Len took up her violin case, and slung the other hand through Richenda's arm. "We'll go by the garden way. It saves time, and thank goodness, there's been no rain, so everything's pretty dry. Let's hope it goes on being fine for the hol! I wonder what we're likely to do!"

This, they were fated not to find out for a while. When they reached Freudesheim, they were met by Anna, Joey's faithful factotum who had been with her ever since her marriage. She held up a warning finger as the pair reached the front door and said, "Not much noise, meiner Kinder. The dear mother very sick has been all night and now she sleeps."

Con and Margot appeared at the door of the dining-room, their faces grave.

"I hope there's nothing badly wrong with Mother," Margot said, her blue eyes shadowed. "Anna says Papa is at the San, but he's coming back shortly. Meantime, she'd bringing our elevenses in here and then we can do what we like so long as we don't make a row."

"We'd best go upstairs and unpack first," Len said, dumping her violin down on the great chest at one side of the hall. "Oh, I do hope Mamma isn't really ill! What did Papa really say about it, Anna?"

118

"Only that he would commit murder on anyone who woke her," Anna said seriously. She had no sense of humour whatsoever, and was given to taking the wildest statements at their face value, greatly to the amusement of the Maynards.

"*That* doesn't tell us anything!" Margot said discontentedly. "Didn't he tell you what was wrong with her at all?"

"Only that she had been sick and had some pain and must sleep now. If you go to unpack, you must be very quiet, mein Vögelein!" Anna replied.

The triplets looked slightly relieved at this. Once or twice in their lives they had known their mother to suffer from a bilious attack. Probably this was the same sort of thing and there was no need to worry.

"Is Ricki in with us or has she a room to herself?" demanded Margot.

"Mamma had an extra bed put into our room for the week-end," Len replied. "Now come on! Tiptoes, Margot! Don't wake Mamma, whatever you do!"

They went upstairs on their tiptoes and presently Richenda found herself in the big room the triplets had shared ever since they came out to the Oberland. It was large, with three beds set between the windows and a fourth set at one side. There was a big wardrobe facing the windows, and a pretty toilet table across one corner. A bookcase filled with books of all kinds faced the windows and there were four chairs. Rugs were scattered over the polished floor and someone had set vases of flowers on the toilet table and the top of the bookcase. The long french windows had curtains of gay flowery cretonne which matched the bedspreads and altogether it would have been hard to find a gayer room for girls anywhere.

"How awfully pretty!" Richenda exclaimed.

"Isn't it?" Len said. "That's your bed, Ricki—there's your case beside it. Get unpacked and then we'll go and get our elevenses. Here's a drawer for you and you can have these pegs in the wardrobe. Now get cracking!—and we'd better not talk much in case we disturb Mamma. Her room's just across the landing on the same side and all the windows are open.

"Do you think we might open her door just the tiniest crack and peep in?" Margot asked.

Len shook her head. "Better not! You know how lightly she sleeps. We'll ask Papa when he comes in. I wonder if we ought to offer to take charge of the kids? Then the Coadjutor could help Anna to cope."

"Oh, I'd love that!" Richenda said in the quick undertone in which they were all talking. "I've never had anything to do with tinies until I met your crowd and I loved them. Perhaps we could take them for a walk?"

"Then we'll put Felix in the reins!" Margot said firmly. "Felicity's as good as can be and Cecil will be in the push-chair. But I, for one, won't take charge of young Felix unless he's safely tethered!"

"We'll harness him and Felicity to the push-chair. They'll like that and they always are careful when Cecil's in it," Len decided. "Finished? Then come on down. Papa should be in soon and we can ask him if we may go and take a dekko at Mamma before we go. Con, you run and tell Anna we'll look after the kids and she can have Rösli."

Con went off and the other three marched into the Speise-saal where Anna had already set a white cloth on a little table by the window. Now she came in bearing a tray laden with glasses of lemonade and a plateful of the delicious sugar cakes she made so well. She was followed by Con whose arm was tucked through her father's.

Richenda had met the doctor at school, so she gave him a beaming smile when he greeted her.

"Hello, Richenda! Glad to see you! Mind you have a good time! And, by the way, how do we shorten that lengthy name of yours?"

"She's Ricki out of school," Len cried as she flung herself on him for a fierce hug—an example followed by Margot while Richenda stared. Even Sue was not given to treating her father that way as a rule.

"Papa, may we go up and peep at Mamma?" Con demanded when order had been restored.

"Not just yet."

"What's wrong with her?" Len demanded

120

"Have your lemonade and take a Leckerli each. You girls are rotten bad hostesses. Here's poor Ricki standing looking longingly at everything and you can't even offer her one little cake!" he said teasingly. "Sit down, Ricki, and help yourself."

They sat down, but when everyone was served, Len began again.

"Papa, what *is* wrong with Mamma? It's nothing bad, is it?"

"That," he said seriously, "is what we don't quite know. Now take those glum looks off your faces, all of you. We're going to find out what it is, and whatever it is, we'll get it put right. I promise you that. Ricki, don't look so worried! We're delighted to have you, child, and mean to show you what we can do in the way of half-term celebrations. Now, you three, I'm going to tell you what we propose for today."

"We've said we'll take the kids out this morning," Len said doubtfully.

"Exactly what I was going to suggest. If those young monkeys are out of the way, Anna and Rösli can cope with the house in comfort. You know, though you won't have Mamma with you today, she and I made quite a few plans and I promised her this morning that we would carry them out to the last dot."

Len gave him a quick glance, but said nothing. Margot, living more on the surface of things, brightened at once.

"She hoped you would do as Len says and take charge of the little ones for the rest of the morning. The Coadjutor can cope with them for the rest of the day. I have to go to Interlaken on business this afternoon, so what about coming with me? I shall leave you at the Beau-Rivage where I'm meeting a man and I expect I'll be pretty busy until four o'clock. You four can have a good prowl about Interlaken and meet me at Génin's pâtisserie at four and I'll treat you to coffee and your own choice of his cakes. Then we must come back and you can put the little ones to bed between you."

"Oh, *stupendous*!" Margot exclaimed. "Do you think we'd have time to take Ricki up to the Harder to see the animals?"

"Better leave that for another day. Why not take her to Unterseen to see the church and the old houses?"

"Oh, jolly good scheme!" Len exclaimed. "Ricki, you'll love it! And there's a wizard fountain there where the old men sit in summer, smoking their meerschaums."

Con lifted her dark eyes to her father's face. "Papa, when may we see Mamma?"

"I'm going upstairs now to see if she's awake while you finish your elevenses. If she is, you may all come up for a few minutes. But I want her to get as much sleep as she can today. She hadn't much last night! But she'll be all right in a day or two, I expect. It wasn't a bad attack this time."

"*This* time? Do you mean she's had others? Len asked anxiously.

"Oh, hang! I didn't mean to alarm you. Yes, she's had two or three, but this has been fairly light. Now don't begin to get anxious. It's probably just her tummy going back on her because she's tired and needs a proper holiday without any worry about you folk. I'm seeing she gets just that when we go to England. We're parking the babies with Auntie Madge and going off by ourselves for a second honeymmon."

"But we did have a holiday—in the new house on the Tiernsee," Margot remarked.

"Ye-es. How much holiday do you think it was for her with the housekeeping to see to and all you lot to worry over?"

The three sat is stricken silence. It had never dawned on them that the family holidays were not much rest for their parents. Jack eyed them curiously. He had made the statement with intention. He felt that at practically fourteen, it was time they realised things of that kind. With six younger than themselves, it was high time the triplets began to take a little more reponsibility for them. Len usually did, but moony Con and insouciant Margot thought very little about it. He rose to his feet.

"I'm off. If it's all right, I'll call you and you can come up. Just remember to come quietly, though. She was feeling rather fragile when I last saw her, and she can't do with wild bears' hugs and squalls of excitement."

He left the room and they heard him taking the stairs, two at a time. He had left the door open and presently they heard him calling to them to come up. The triplets rushed ahead. Richenda followed much more slowly. She wondered if she ought to be at Freudesheim when Mrs. Maynard was unwell. But if she didn't stay, where else could she go? The school was closed and she hadn't enough money to go to a hotel, even if anyone would allow it which she rather thought they would not. She must just remain and be as little trouble as possible.

By the time she reached the open doorway, the triplets had kissed their mother and been kissed by her. She was lying back on her big French pillows, looking round inquiringly.

"Where's Richenda?" she demanded. "You surely haven't left her alone downstairs? I want to see her."

"I'm here," Richenda said shyly from the doorway.

Joey sat up, her long black pigtails dangling over her shoulders, and held out her hands. "Come along and be kissed and welcomed! Oh, my poor lamb! What a welcome to give you! But I really couldn't help it. I didn't *want* to be sick!"

"What have you been doing to be sick?" Len asked sternly.

"Oh, this and that!" Her mother released Richenda and lay back again. "Papa says I'm tired and need a rest. I expect that's the top and bottom of it."

"Are you *sure* you're feeling better now?" Con asked.

"Much better. In fact, I'm developing an appetite once more. I'm looking forward to a little something for lunch. But *not* tripe! Don't anyone dare to so much as show me *that*!" She laughed. "I could fancy a little cold chicken with one of Anna's rolls. And some of her baked custard to finish with. What about it, Jack?"

"We'll see by the time it's ready," he said. "I know you're one of the world's marvels when it comes to making a recovery. In fact, you have even Mary-Lou beat at that particular game. But you can't try your tummy too much at first."

"Oh, very well! And now, you folk, I'm sorry, but you'll

have to make up your minds to do without me for today, I'm afraid. Tomorrow, too, I understand."

"You're certainly staying in bed tomorrow," her husband told her severely. "And serve you right for getting up a scare of this kind! We'll see what you're like on Monday. Sunday in bed will probably put a stop to your little antics!"

"Can you see me? You know as well as I do that I loathe my bed except at the proper time and you don't keep me here a moment longer than necessary. I feel pretty well all right now, but I'll stay where I am till Sunday morning, just to ease your silly mind. You do get into such a flap over nothing!"

But the look that passed between the pair of them took all the tartness out of her retort.

"Oh, how jolly lucky the Maynards are to have such a father and mother!" Richenda thought. "Why must *I* have a father like mine?"

Joey's quick eyes saw her change of expression and she guessed what the girl was thinking and promptly tried to turn her thoughts into a happier channel.

"I've planned some glorious trips for you folks," she remarked. "No, never mind what they are now. You know what's happening today and you'll know about the rest as it comes. Have you had your elevenses?"

"Yes, we had them before we came upstairs," Len replied. "Don't bother about the little ones, either. We're going to take them out in a minute or two and we're taking the reins and harnessing the twins to the push-chair."

"Good for you! Then I haven't a thing to worry about and I can go to sleep again quite comfortably. Mind you don't stay out too long, though. Lunch at midday, remember, or you'll miss your train and then Papa will have to go without you and you won't like *that*!" She spoke with conviction.

"We shan't!" Margot cried. "We'll be back in heaps of time!"

Con bent down for another kiss. "You're a bad woman to give us such a fright, but we'll forgive you as you're getting better."

"Such condescension!" Joey mocked. "O.K. You three

124

can scoot off now and get the babies ready for their walk. Ricki, you can get ready and then hunt up the reins. You'll probably find them hanging up in the cloakroom. Oh, by the way, going to Interlaken is an expensive business, so here's a small contribution for each of you. Now scram! If I have a lazy time today and tomorrow, I'll be up on Sunday and quite fit for Monday's show, and I jolly well mean to be! *Out*, all of you!"

She handed an envelope to each of them, pulled down her pillow till she was lying nearly flat, turned on her side and shut her eyes and took no further notice of anyone.

"She doesn't look too bad," Con said as they went to their bedroom to open the envelopes. "She's paler than usual and her eyes look a bit smudgy, but that's all. She'll soon be all right again." She had been opening her envelope carefully as she spoke. Now she drew out a little sheaf of notes with smothered squeal of delight. "Oh, goody! She's given me twenty-five francs! Oh, isn't she a dear darling of the mother!"

"She's a complete poppet!" Margot agreed. "What shall we bring her from Interlaken?"

"Better wait and see what we can find," Len said cautiously. "Mine's twenty-five, too! I know, let's ask Papa if there's any book she specially wants and we can club together and get it—if we see it," she added prudently.

Richenda alone remained silent. She stood, holding the money and wondering how Mrs. Maynard could possibly know that she had very little indeed. Her father had allowed her the minimum of pocket-money and the minimum for her school bank. With Christmas coming at the end of term, she had been afraid to draw much for the weekend and her purse was very lean.

She blinked back the tears in her eyes as she thought of the kindness. "Oh," she breathed to herself, "Mrs. Maynard really is almost the kindest, dearest person I ever knew! If ever I can do anything for her, I will, no matter what it is!"

Then she remembered that Joey *had* asked her to find the reins, so she tucked the notes away in her bag and went off to hunt them up, her mind full of good intentions.

Chapter XIV

Joey has a Crack at It

The trip to Interlaken began with a breathtaking descent from the Görnetz Platz to the plain below. Jack Maynard shut his engine off, jammed his brakes on and took her slowly and carefully down, but Richenda held her breath most of the way. Never, in all her life, had she seen such a road, twisting and turning and zigzagging the whole way and going down, down, down, till once or twice she thought the car would stand on its bonnet and they would all be flung out.

Arrived in Interlaken, Jack turned them out, asked them if they had all the money they needed, cautioned them about looking before they crossed the road, which brought unseemly hoots from his daughters, and a firm reminder from Margot that they had lived in Switzerland for *years* now and knew all about it, and then went off to his interview, leaving them to their own devices.

The triplets firmly took charge and introduced Richenda to the floral clock at the Kursaal, and then the spot from which the best view of the Jungfrau is obtained. They then caught a tram which took them across the Aare to Unterseen where they pointed out the various sights, before coming back on another tram and settling down to shopping. The book for Joey was found and Richenda bought her a tiny phial of perfume. She also invested in sweets to be shared by all of them and the triplets, not to be outdone, chose slabs of chocolate. A tiny dolly was bought for Felicity, a monkey-up-the-stick for Felix, and a china swan to float in her bath for Cecil. Then they had to run to be at the pâtisserie on time.

Jack treated them to cups of coffee with what Richenda, in a letter to Sue Mason, described as "positive featherbeds of whipped cream" floating on top. Then they had another race home—or rather, so far as the mountain path was concerned, a slow crawl. But once they had reached the shelf, Jack trod on his accelerator for he was late for his visit to the

San and must decant the girls at Freudesheim before he could make it.

They found the patient awake after sleeping sweetly most of the day, and very much better. Joey never had much colour, but now her cheeks were faintly pink and the smudges had disappeared from under her eyes. She talked of getting up next day, but when next day came, found she was under orders to stay where she was under pain of not being allowed to join Monday's expedition which, it seemed, was to be the crown of the weekend.

"But what will you do with the girls?" she demanded.

"The girls will be all right. Biddy is taking them to Berne for the day."

Joey chuckled, "You know, Jack, this isn't at all the sort of half-term Professor Fry envisaged for his bad daughter! I wish I could get hold of the man and try to talk a little sense into him! He's really going the right way to make Ricki hate him for the rest of her days. Doesn't the silly idiot *see* that!"

"Evidently not. Look here, Joey, you'll have to see if you can do something with that kid. She can't be allowed to go on as she's doing. It's bad for her. As for the Professor——"

"You leave him to me. We're going to England shortly, aren't we? *And* to London where we'll be part of the time and he lives fairly near. *I'll* sort him!" quoth Jo darkly.

"You'll do no such thing!" her husband retorted, moved by a well founded fear of what she might elect to say if they ever met. "You're going to London for an overhaul. Provided there's nothing really wrong, you and I are going off on our second honeymoon with the babies parked with Madge, and nothing to worry about—except how long the cash will hold out," he added, grinning.

"But Jack, have you considered that we are the parents of nine healthy youngsters? Rather late to talk of a second honeymoon, surely?"

"Never mind that! It's high time you had a decent holiday. You've scarcely been away from the family since the triplets came, except when you've added to 'em. You're having one now, and a good one!"

"Bully! O.K. I'll play ball. I'll stay in bed till tea-time, but

I am getting up then for an hour or two. I really feel quite fit and it's only to please you I'm staying here for the day."

"We'll see. Now, here's your new book. I hope you enjoy it. I'm off to breakfast. Biddy said she and Eugen would be calling for the crowd at nine, so I told Anna breakfast at eight sharp."

Richenda enjoyed Berne even more than Interlaken. "Auntie Biddy", as the triplets called her, knew the old city very thoroughly and was an excellent guide. She showed them the very pick of the sights and fed them lusciously on typical Bernese dishes at the Kornhauskellar. They arrived back by seven o'clock to find Joey up in her bedroom and looking herself again.

On Sunday morning she was down as usual to accompany her children to Mass. Jack took them in the car and they dropped Richenda at the Protestant church on their way. In the afternoon, duly warned, he called the triplets and took them and the little ones off for a trip in the car, but Joey claimed Richenda.

"Ricki, you won't mind staying to keep me company, will you? You've been my guest for nearly three days and we've never had a decent talk."

Richenda was quite agreeable. She was growing very fond of her hostess and even the brief interviews they had had, confirmed her in her belief that Mrs. Maynard was, above all things, an understanding woman. She had no idea what she was in for!

When the rest had left the house, Joey marched her off to the salon where a big wood fire was burning in the open fireplace. Most houses in Switzerland are heated by closed stoves or central heating, but Joey had claimed that she must have at least *one* friendly fire to look at in winter, so they had put in a fireplace in the salon.

"Pull up that chair," Joey said. "Settle yourself and start in on these!" producing from behind the cushion in her own chair a box of chocolates. "And now tell me, how do you like school?"

Richenda talked for an hour on end about it! By that time, Mrs. Maynard had gathered that she loved the Chalet School, was very happy, and had every intention of going ahead for all she was worth. Then she forgot and slipped.

"I don't intend to give HIM any opportunity of saying it's doing me no good and taking me away and sending me somewhere else a second time!" she said bitterly.

Joey seized her opportunity with both hands. "Him?" she said, a gentle interest in her tone that yet was somehow scarifying. "And who may you mean by that?"

Richenda reddened and looked embarrassed. "Well—my father," she muttered.

Joey sat up and faced her squarely. "Look here, Ricki! I loathe preaching, but you're driving me to it. Why do you speak of your father like that? It isn't exactly respectful—*or* affectionate, is it?"

Richenda would have given worlds to look away, but something in the beautiful black eyes fronting her, kept her own steadily on them. "I—I don't feel that way!" she blurted out at last.

"Why not?" Joey carefully kept the interest in her tone.

"Well—you know how he's treated me—taking me away from Maggie's—and——"

"But I thought you loved being here and fully understood that you were getting a far better education at the Chalet School? And you know, Ricki, if you really mean to go in for ceramics as you've said, you'll need a very thorough education. You'll be mixing with cultured and cultivated people and you don't want to feel at a loss. Then, you ought to be able to read other than English books on the subject and that you'll do best by knowing other languages inside out. You see that?"

"I—I suppose so," Richenda stammered.

"Then in that case isn't it rather a good thing that he took you from a second-rate school and sent you to one where you really do get good teaching? I ought to know," she added with a grin. "I had five solid years of it myself."

"I—yes, I think so. But you know, Mrs. Maynard, I don't think that was the real idea. He wanted to punish me and punish me hard. He said so! And he's gone *on* punishing me! He wouldn't let me go with the others to the Valais for that reason. Of course, I'm having a gorgeous time here," she added hurriedly, feeling that her last remark might sound rather insulting, "but he didn't know that would happen. What he was really out to do was to make me miserable."

Joey considered this in silence, praying inwardly for wisdom. "No," she said at last. "I think you're wrong there, Ricki. What he really wanted was to ensure that in future you would obey him about the Chinese Room. But I also think he took the chance to give you a better education than you were getting. After all," she added reasonably, "he's a man of considerable learning, and if he took the slightest interest in what you were doing, he must have realised that St. Margaret's wasn't good enough for a clever girl—and especially, his own daughter."

"He always went over my school reports with me," Richenda admitted honestly.

"Exactly! And there's another point of view as well. You know, if any of *my* girls went on deliberately disobeying a clear order as you seem to have done, I should certainly feel very angry with them."

"I don't think you would," Richenda said startlingly, so far as her audience was concerned. "Oh, I don't mean you wouldn't be vexed. But I do believe you'd try to find out just *why* it happened. He won't. And he doesn't seem to see that I can't help it, any more than *he* could! Honestly, Mrs. Maynard, I can't! It—it's *part* of me! And mustn't I get it from him? Nanny says my mother was never awfully keen about his china."

Joey nearly gasped. She had not expected Richenda to be far enough advanced to reason all this out for herself. She looked at her with a certain respect and vowed again that when she was in England she would wangle an opportunity to meet Professor Fry and take it up with him. Aloud, she said. "Yes, I think you're right on both counts. I certainly *should* want to know what was at the bottom of it all. Equally, I'm *sure* it's part of your heritage from your father."

"Yes, well, he doesn't understand—and won't! He just gives me an order and says I've got to obey it, and that's finish! And Nanny can't understand, either. She says I'm a naughty girl and deserve all I get."

Joey laughed. "I can just hear her saying it!—have another choc, Ricki?—but what I'm trying to get at, my lamb, is that if your father isn't trying to understand *you*, neither are you trying to understand *him*. It cuts both ways."

"O-oh!" said Richenda, and was silent. She hadn't thought of it in that light.

"Well, it is so, isn't it!" Joey insisted.

"I—I suppose so." Then she added suddenly, "but *you* would understand—you *do* understand!"

"Yes, but in the first place, *my* great interest is people. As a writer, I try to get at the reasons behind people's behaviour. *His* great interest is things which don't behave, one way or the other. It makes a difference. And then," Joey added with an infectious grin, "I'll bet I'm a good many years younger than your father!"

"Oh, yes, you're *years* younger!" Richenda assured her. "I know he and Mother were married for nearly ten years before I came and Nanny once said that she was so glad when Mother married him because she was much too sweet to be an old maid. She was twenty-eight when they married."

"I see. Yes, that means they weren't *young* parents. But Dr. Jack and I *were*. I wasn't quite twenty-one when the triplets arrived. Our birthdays are in the same month, you know. They're at the beginning and I'm at the end. Dearie me! When I think what an infant I was at that time!" And Joey broke into laughter.

Richenda was surprised into laughing with her. When they had sobered down, Joey eyed her carefully and added, "And what sort of letters have you been writing home to your father, Ricki? Nice, friendly ones, telling him all the news?"

Richenda went scarlet again. "How did you know? I haven't! I wouldn't have written at all if I hadn't had to!"

"I guessed as much! You've been keeping up your resentment at the way he treated you, and you've let him see it by what you write to him. My dear girl, how can you expect him to loosen up if that's the way you've been behaving? Of

131

course, he feels that you don't care two hoots for his punishment so far, and that's making him more determined than ever to *make* you care! I'm sorry, my lamb, but I'm afraid you'll have to conquer that stubborn pride of yours and cave in a little. The consequences if you don't mayn't be at all pleasant!"

"What do you mean?" Richenda demanded sharply.

"Only that if he thinks you're getting a kick out of the Chalet School and having a jolly good time here, he may resolve to remove you. You told me you were working hard so that he shouldn't have any reason for taking you away. But if he thinks you aren't improving in *character*, it's just as likely to make him do it as if you slacked and didn't do a stroke of work."

"I didn't think of that!" Richenda exclaimed, aghast at the idea.

"Have you thought at all about it—except your own side?" Joey demanded.

Richenda was silent once more. Really, Mrs. Maynard had a very uncomfortable way of getting at you! She didn't like to own it, but she was seeing her own conduct in quite a new light. She still felt her father had been very unfair to her. But on the other hand, had she been quite fair to him?

"What do you want me to do!" she asked, so bluntly that Joey, who was using the pause to choose a chocolate, started and dropped the box.

They had to scrabble all round for the chocolates, but when they sat up again, Mrs. Maynard had her answer ready.

"You must try to forgive your father. Oh, yes, I agree that you have something to forgive, but so has he!"

"Do you mean I've got to say I'm sorry?" Richenda asked, appalled.

"You can either do that—or write him a decent letter for once," Joey said promptly. "You haven't written home yet, have you?"

"Yes, I did it after Church."

"May I see it?"

For reply, Richenda got up and brought her letter from

the chest where she had put it after lunch. Joey carefully opened it murmuring, "We can stick up the envelope with sellotape. Pity to waste the stamp!" Then she read it, and between dismay and amusement, was speechless for a moment or two.

"Dear Father," Richenda had written, "Thank you for your last letter. I hope your cold is better. The weather here has been very fine ever since the thunderstorm a week or two ago. I was sixth in form for the last fortnight. I am staying with Mrs. Maynard, and yesterday our history mistress took the Maynard girls and me to Berne. We saw a number of historical buildings." Here followed a list. "No one could give me any preparation as they were all too busy. I am reading *Mansfield Park* which is part of our literature for this year."

Here, Joey, who knew how much Miss Richenda was enjoying *Mansfield Park*, looked across at her to say with mock severity, "Yes, a nasty holiday task you find that, don't you?" Then she went on.

"I am also learning some long speeches from our Shakespeare play. I think this is all the news I have for you. Richenda."

Joey read the effusion through three times. Then she handed it to the writer.

"I'd like you to read it aloud to me, please."

With a startled glance, Richenda meekly took it and began. Halfway through, she stopped dead and looked at Joey. "*Oh*! It *is* rather a brute!"

"Well, now you know what to do!" Joey popped a final chocolate into her mouth and got up saying in rather muffled tones, "I'm going to see about tea. The rest will be back presently. No; you stay where you are." Then she marched out of the room, leaving a rather stricken Richenda behind her.

When she came back, the letter had vanished, but there were one or two paper ashes on the hearth. She had the wisdom to say nothing, and as the family arrived a minute or two later, no more was ever said. But before she went to bed that night, a slightly embarrassed Richenda came to ask if

133

she might have the sellotape to stick up the envelope again, and the three sheets she showed Joey were a distinct improvement on her first effort.

"So," said the lady later on when she was telling Jack about the afternoon's events, "I seem to have butted in to some purpose where Ricki is concerned. *Now*, whether you like it or not, I'm having a go at her father while we're in England. Ricki is much too decent a girl to be spoilt because a stupid professor hasn't the sense to see that she's not the type to do much for mere bossing! I'll make him see it before I've done with him, though, or my name isn't Josephine Mary Maynard!"

Joey roused everyone at half-past six the next morning, but refused to reveal her plans for the last full day of the weekend until everyone was seated at the breakfast table. Her announcement that the girls were to have their much longed for trip to the Valais was met with shrieks of delight.

A quarter past eight saw them packed into the car and ready to set off on the long journey through the valleys and villages of Switzerland to the Valais region. They visited several of that pictureque area's towns and villages, but, as Joey remarked, it could be no more than a whistle-stop tour when you were trying to fit it all into one day.

The triplets and Richenda were thrilled with everything that day; their lunch of typically Valaisian dishes, their first glimpse of the majestic Matterhorn, the historic towns nestling amongst the vineyards and apricot orchards that are a feature of the Valais, and finally, the majestic town of Sion, built on two hills, where the girls managed to buy small gifts for everyone as mementos of their trip.

They returned to Freudesheim long after it was dark, and as they crept upstairs to bed, Richenda summed it up for all of them. "Thank you so much, Mrs. Maynard!" she whispered. "I've had a glorious time." Joey grinned at the four tired girls and chased them up the stairs.

Chapter XV

A TERRIBLE ACCIDENT

JOEY left the four to sleep next morning. They had had a full day and a late one, and she had no wish to be called to account by Matron for returning the girls to school worn out by all they had done. It was ten o'clock when Len and Richenda finally made their appearance for breakfast, Len quite calm, and Richenda inclined to be very apologetic. Joey laughed the apologies away.

"Don't be so silly. If I'd wanted you to be early, I could have called you, couldn't I? Sit down, my lamb, and wrap yourself round that!"

She passed Richenda a bowl of cereal and cream as she spoke. "Wire in! Len, are Con and Margot up yet?"

"Margot is. Con isn't," Len returned, spooning up corn-flakes and cream at a great rate. "What are we going to do today?"

"Nothing—I mean you aren't going anywhere. Papa has had a rather worrying business letter, and in any case, you have to be back at school by eighteen o'clock, so I thought a walk this morning, and a quiet afternoon reading or playing games, and Kaffee und Kuchen with Anna's special cream cakes."

Margot arrived at this point and Con followed ten minutes later. Thereafter, they followed the programme she had outlined and spent a quiet day. But shortly before they went over to the school, Joey called her three girls into the study.

"I have some rather sad news for you folk," she said, as they gathered round her. "I'm very, very sorry, but Papa and I won't be here for your birthday."

Her daughters stared at her unmitigated dismay in their faces.

"Not here for our birthday?" Len gasped. "But, Mamma! *Why?*"

"Is it something to do with the letter Papa had this morning?" Con queried.

"But how can we celebrate if *you* aren't here?" Margot demanded.

"If you'll all try to keep quiet for just two minutes," Joey said, "I'll tell you." Then she melted. "Oh, my poor lambs! I hate it as much as you do, but it just can't be helped this time. Now, listen with all your ears, for we haven't much time."

They had sat down and the three faces were turned to hers—rather mournful faces, as she went on.

"You knew that Papa and I were going to England on business connected with the two Sans. A letter came from Uncle Jem this morning and he wants Papa to go this week, so that they can go into things before the actual conference, which takes place on Wednesday of next week. Some of the rules governing the arrangements for the San up here, and the one in the Welsh mountains, are coming up for alteration. Uncle Jem and Papa have their own ideas about this and Uncle Jem wants to have everything ready and clearly set out for the conference. It really is a wise move on his part, and Papa and I both agree that he must go."

"But *you* won't be at the conference, any more than Auntie Madge will," Margot pointed out. "Couldn't you just stay over for the birthday and then go to Auntie Madge's after?"

"I could—but I don't want to," Joey said quietly. "I don't feel like that long journey on my own. You people know that I haven't been very well lately. That's one reason why I'm going with Papa. He wants me to see Sir James Talbot."

Len sprang up, terror in her eyes. "Mamma! Are you ill—really ill, I mean?"

"I hope not—in fact, I don't really think so. But I've had two or three sick turns lately and a little pain," Joey said. "You girls are quite old enough to realise that when the usual remedies aren't doing much about it, I'd be all sorts of an idiot if I didn't have it seen to. But I don't think, and neither does Papa, that it's anything very much. And when it's all over and Sir James has given me some medicine and told me to run away and play, that's exactly what Papa and I mean to do," she added, cheerfully.

The terror faded from their eyes.

"Papa did say something about it at the beginning of the

hol," Margot said slowly. "I'd forgotten, though, we've had so much to do. Are you *sure* it isn't much?"

"Certain! When have I ever lied to you?" Joey asked calmly.

"*Never!*" Len said with emphasis. "If you didn't want us to know anything, you've told us to stop asking for you weren't going to say. But you've never put us off with yarns. That's why we can trust you."

"Very well, then. And Auntie Hilda is giving you a party in the evening on Saturday, and Anna is sending in your usual cake. Presents are waiting and will duly arrive—unless you do anything so evil, you don't deserve to have them," Joey added with a peal of laughter.

"We'll be angels!" Margot cried. Then she added anxiously, "Papa will tell us if—if— —"

"Of course!" Joey spoke quickly. "And don't you start imagining horrors! I'll write to you myself, once I've seen Sir James. And I promise to tell you the exact truth," she added. "Oh, just one thing! Don't say a word about all this to anyone else except Auntie Hilda or Matey. *They* know, of course."

"O.K, we won't say a word," Len promised.

"What are we to say to the girls if they ask us?" Con inquired.

"You can tell them that we've got rid of all our responsibilities and gone off for a second honeymoon," Joey said with a chuckle. "It's no business of theirs, anyway. If they persist, you can tell them that."

Len had thought of something. "What about Mary-Lou?"

"I don't want even Mary-Lou to know any more. Now, my precious lambs, it's high time you were thinking of going back to school. Run and call Ricki, Len, and you two get your coats and caps on. I rather think I hear a coach coming down the road and Auntie Hilda won't love any of us if you're late."

They did as she told them and no more was said. But Richenda was rather startled by the way the three clung to their mother when she kissed them good-bye. She waved them off in the end, promising to look in on the morrow, and they went flying when Con, with a glance at the clock, cried that it was just on eighteen o'clock and they had one minute to be at school on time.

Luckily for them, their own crowd had so much to say about their holiday, that no one noticed that they were much quieter than usual. Vb had had the trip of their lives, to judge by their clatter, and they enlarged on it for the rest of the evening.

Joey went off on the Thursday, having faithfully kept her promise and called her triplets out of school in the middle of the morning so that she could say good-bye. And when afternoon school began, there was a summons to Hall for everyone to hear the news that she had left the MS. of the Christmas play before she went, and after prep and Abendessen that night, the school would hear it.

But though the triplets were delighted, especially when the parts were given out next day and they found that each had a "speaking" part for the first time, they still remained quieter than usual and Richenda, at least, wondered about it. She knew better than the rest of the form about Joey's attacks.

On the following Monday, a letter arrived addressed to "The Misses Maynard" and when the Head heard of it, she summoned them to her private sitting-room and left them to read it. Joey had seen Sir James Talbot on the Saturday morning, and if his report was not as good as it might have been, it was nothing to worry about. She had displaced an organ slightly, which meant an operation to correct it, but Sir James promised that she would be only a short time in the nursing home and when it was over she would be as fit as ever.

"So, you see, no one need be upset about me after all," she wrote. "Now forget about it and put your backs into your work *and* play, and be ready to welcome us both home exactly four weeks from today. That's when we expect to arrive."

Joey told them that she was going into the nursing home on the Wednesday but the operation would not take place till Sunday morning. Their father would let them know as soon as it was over and they weren't to worry.

"A much better thing will be to pray for me and remember me at Mass on Sunday," she wrote. "Papa will ring up the school in the afternoon, so don't expect any news before then. But it'll be all right. It's quite a minor thing and I've been perfectly fit since that last attack at half-term.

"Now I must finish. Give my love to everyone who wants it and heaps for your own precious selves. Auntie Madge will write on Sunday night. She and Papa and Uncle Jem will all be in London so as to get all the news at once."

"Well, I suppose it's not too bad," Len sighed, as she folded the letter, "but Saturday and Sunday morning are going to be hectic days! It's all very well to say 'Don't worry', but we can't help it! Not with Mamma!"

However, by Saturday afternoon, something else had happened which took their thoughts almost completely off their mother for a few hours, and by the time they could have begun to worry badly, Jack's message had come through. The operation was well over and a complete success.

On the Friday morning, Matron bustled into the staff-room before Frühstück. "I'm having a teeth inspection this morning, everyone. I'll begin with VIa and go right through the school. Tomorrow, anyone who needs attention will come down with me to Berne. I've booked with Herr von Francius, and he's giving us the whole day after twelve o'clock. Who has first lesson with VIa?"

"The Head." Miss Derwent said with a glance at the timetable.

"Good! I'll just go and have a word with her!" And Matron departed to issue her commands.

In the end, fifteen girls were found to need Herr von Francius's attentions, among them, Mary-Lou Trelawney, Len, Richenda and Rosamund Lilley. Miss Ferrars and Miss Wilmot, who were free on Saturday, offered to act as escort with Matron and the party set off by the eight o'clock train with the prospect of some trouble to be followed by some pleasure. The two mistresses had promised to show them one or two sights that would be fresh to most of them, and they would not return until the eighteen o'clock train.

They got off in plenty of time, and even the prospective victims enjoyed the journey down to Interlaken and then on to Berne which they reached by eleven. They went to a café where they were well-known for coffee and afterwards, armed with the toothbrushes they all had to bring, they cleaned their teeth, and finally set off for the quiet street where Herr von Francius lived.

They were about a quarter of an hour before their time, and he had one other patient to deal with before he turned his attention to the school. This was a lady with a small boy of six or seven. She stared when the girls marched in and sat down quietly with books and magazines they had brought with them. The boy stared even harder.

"Mommy, what are they going to do?" he demanded in a shrill treble.

"Hush, Junior. It's rude to make remarks," she returned in a tone which made the two mistresses and Matron raise their eyebrows. She so obviously did not expect him to take any notice of what she said.

They were quite right. Junior merely gaped at the party and then inquired with a giggle, "Will they all cry? I guess they'll all *yell*!"

"Junior! Do be quiet!" his mother implored. "Why don't you look at the pictures in one of those magazines?"

He took no notice of her. Instead, he walked round the room, staring hard at each girl. Mary-Lou said later that she yearned to take him by the shoulders and shove him down on a chair.

Miss Wilmot went one better. She muttered to her two companions in rapid German that it would give her all the pleasure in the world to turn him over her knee and administer the spanking he needed!

The girls were boiling inside, but they knew better than to take any notice. He glared at them, ignoring his mother's feeble commands to come and sit down beside her and keep quiet.

A moment later, finding that his comments seemed to rouse no one, he ventured further. Rosamund's long thick pigtail had fallen over her shoulder. Suddenly, he darted at her, gripped it, and gave it a good tug. Rosamund cried out and Richenda grabbed him and pulled him off.

"Go away and leave us alone, you rude little wretch!" she exclaimed as she pushed him away.

Before anyone could do anything, he snatched something from his pocket, his face red with rage. He aimed the object straight at Richenda's face and squeezed. A small jet shot out, catching her in the eyes and at once a wild scream rang through the room.

"Oh, my eyes—my eyes!"

Matron was beside her in a moment, handkerchief in hand. The girls sprung round and Nancy Wilmot and Kathie Ferrars caught the now scared child and were gripping him fast.

"You little beast!" Miss Wilmot exclaimed. "Give me that thing at once!" And she opened his fist forcibly and snatched from it a small squirt. A drop or two of whatever he had had in it still lingered, and she looked at it anxiously, for Richenda was moaning terribly. It was clearly not water he had used. She lifted it to her nose and choked.

"Matron! We want oil!" she gasped. "It's some kind of ammonia!"

By this time the boy was screaming lustily and trying to kick Kathie Ferrars who was still clutching him. His mother was exclaiming and bewailing his naughtiness and the girls were all watching Matron who had guided Richenda to a seat and was stooping over her. Richenda still uttered those heart-rending moans.

"Oh, my eyes! They're burning out! They're burning out!"

Nancy Wilmot shoved the squirt into the hand of Mary-Lou who was standing nearest, and swung round to seek the dentist and oil when he burst into the room.

Between them, he and Matron got Richenda into another room and he produced an emulgent and they began to bathe the poor eyes. But whatever the child had used, it was not ordinary ammonia and she still kept up her sharp cries.

"She must go the Augenklinik!" he said at last. "This needs expert treatment. Bitte, meine Frau, wait a moment. I will bring my car round."

The mother of the boy tried to take him and escape. Mary-Lou, however, shut the door and leaned her back against it.

"Oh, no, you don't!" she said grimly. "You'll stay here until we know something definite and answer for that imp of Satan! If he's blinded Richenda, you're going to know all about it!"

"How can you be so cruel?" the woman sobbed. "He didn't do it on purpose."

"Rubbish!" Mary-Lou retorted, while the mistresses got the others to order again. "He took deliberate aim at her."

Miss Wilmot came to back up Mary-Lou with her authority. "What is your name?" she demanded.

"I'm Mrs. Van Allen," the lady sobbed. "Oh, dear! Mr. Van Allen will be real vexed with Junior when he hears. Please let that lady know we'll pay all expenses. I know he would wish me to promise that!"

"*Pay*!" Nancy said in blistering tones. "If that poor child is robbed of her sight, how much *money* do you imagine can pay for *that*?"

Mrs. Van Allen only sobbed incoherently.

"What *was* the stuff the little wretch used?" Kathie Ferrars asked, releasing him as she spoke. "If we knew that, we might be able to do something."

"Oh, I don't know!" Mrs. Van Allen sobbed. "Oh, dear! Junior's crying terribly. Junior, my darling——"

"He's only screaming with temper," Mary-Lou said calmly. "He wants a good smacking!"

"He—he's never been smacked in his life!" his mother cried indignantly.

"It's never too late to mend," Nancy Wilmot assured her. She descended on the boy who yelled as if he feared she meant to administer it then and there. "Stop that silly screaming at once and tell us what you used!"

"Shan't!" he howled. "Mommy! Mommy! I hate them! Make them let us go!"

His mother looked round at the stern faces of everyone and collapsed into tears again. "Oh, *Junior*!" she wailed. "What will Poppa say to you?"

Len came up to the group, tears streaming down her face. "Oh, Miss Ferrars! Will Ricki never see again?" she wept.

"We'll hope it won't come to that, Len," Miss Ferrars said quickly. "Here's Matron now!" as the door opened and Matron came in. But one look at her face told them that she had no good news for them.

"Whatever it was, it wasn't just ammonia," she said. "Herr von Francius is getting his car and we're taking her to the Eye Hospital. You'll have to wait here with the girls until I get back. Herr von Francius will return at once, of course." Then she looked round. "Where's that boy?"

He had taken the opportunity to scuttle to his mother and get behind her. Matron saw him, however.

"Come out!" she commanded in tones that allowed no disobedience. Even the staff had been known to shiver in their shoes when she spoke like that. He crept out from behind his mother and stood there, terrified.

"What was that stuff?" she demanded.

"It was a bottle I—found in—the garage at—our hotel," he confessed shakily.

"There's just a drop or two left in the squirt," Miss Wilmot said, her own voice none too steady.

Mary-Lou produced it and Matron took it and sniffed. "Yes, we'll take it with us. They may know what it is and it will help them to know what to do. I must go back to her."

"Is—is she in much pain?" Mary-Lou asked fearfully though she still kept her post at the door.

"A good deal, I'm afraid. She moans all the time, poor child. However, they will probably be able to do something to relieve that at the hospital. But what damage has been done to the eyes, I can't say of course." She swung round on the terrified Mrs. Van Allen. "This is *your* fault! *You* are to blame! If you'd brought that child up properly, this would never have happened. I hope you'll learn your lesson or you may have even more to regret over him later." With which she turned on her heel and swept out, leaving Mrs. Van Allen gaping after her, open mouthed.

Chapter XVI

PROFESSOR FRY

PROFESSOR FRY was sitting in his study, Richenda's last letter before him on the desk. He was reading it for the second time and as he read, he nodded.

"At last! The school is evidently beginning to take hold now. What an obstinate young woman she is! Not a word of repentance from her all these weeks! And even now, she hasn't said she's sorry. Still, it is distinctly better." Involuntarily, his eyes sought the photograph of Richenda's mother which stood at the corner of the desk. "Oh, my dear," he said, "I wish you'd lived to bring her up. I could have dealt with a boy, but a girl is beyond me."

The door opened and Nanny entered. She held out her hand, showing a cable. "It's from Switzerland," she said briefly.

"*What*?" He snatched it from her and tore it open. The telephone had gone wrong and the men had not yet been to repair it. He spread it out and read it. "Come at once. Richenda bad accident. Annersley."

He read it over and over and gradually a sick feeling of fear took possession of him. He passed it across to Nanny who was still standing there. "Here! You'd best read it!" he said harshly.

Nanny read it slowly. Then she dropped it with a cry. "My Richenda!" She glared at him. "What have they been doing with her? Letting her climb some of them ice mountains and have a bad fall? I'm going at once!"

He made a big effort and recovered his self-possession. "Very well. Have those men been to put the phone right yet? No? Then I must go next door and ring the airport. You go and get on with the packing. We're flying on the first plane possible."

He left the room on the word and Nanny bundled off after him. "Tell Mrs. Mason while you're busy!" she called as he hurried down the garden path. "Likely the doctor can tell us something to help. I'll be packing and seeing to things."

She set to work at once. By the time Professor Fry came back with the news that if they hurried, they could just make the night plane to Zurich, two cases were ready; the silver had been locked away; dust-sheets had been thrown over the drawing-room furniture and the house was beginning to grow cold.

Mrs. Mason arrived ten minutes later to take the keys and promise to keep an eye on things. She handed the Professor an envelope.

"This is from George. He says the banks are closed, so you may not have enough money in the house. Luckily, he cashed a cheque this morning, so we had this handy. We can settle up later. And Professor, if you want me, let me know, and I'll come out at once. And cable us as soon as you know what's wrong. We shall be very anxious until we hear."

"Nanny will see to it," he said dully.

"What are you doing about the Chinese Room? Have you let the police know?"

"Damn the Chinese Room!" he said deliberately. He felt like that now. If it had not been for that, he would never had sent Richenda so far away and she would have been safe at home with him. If anything serious had happened, how was he ever to face it?

In those moments, Professor Fry paid heavily for his unkind treatment of his only child. All his resentment at her continued impenitence was gone, overlaid by the awful anxiety that was racking him. If only he should find when he reached the school that she was safe, he felt he could whistle every single one of his beloved porcelains down the wind and think no more of them.

Mrs. Mason eyed him keenly. She had a shrewd idea how he felt. "Don't lose hope," she said gently. "They've sent for you and I think if the worst had happened, they would have waited to write. Now, off you go and don't worry about anything. I'll lock up and turn the water, electricity and gas off."

Nanny appeared, and spoke to her master without any of her customary respect. She was blaming him bitterly for whatever it was that had befallen her nursling. "What are we to do about the telephone men?"

"Don't you worry about that," Mrs. Mason said briskly. "I'll wait till they've been. Better get off. The doctor's outside with the car. He's running you up to the airport. Nanny, you'll let me know how Richenda goes on?"

"I'll let you know, ma'am," Nanny replied as she picked up her case. "But likely she's in hospital and they may not let me see her." Her voice shook as she spoke out her present great fear.

"The Professor will see to that, won't you, Professor?" Mrs. Mason said.

"Anything—anything!" he replied hastily, snatching up his case and going out to the car.

They were fairly soon at the airport, for the doctor knew all the short cuts, so that they had plenty of time to do everything. At last they were seated in the plane, and then began the worst time for Professor Fry. Up to this moment he had had to occupy himself with all the arrangements, so that he had had very little time to think. But now, there was nothing to do but sit there. He went back over the time since the trouble over the Khang-he vase. He told himself that he had been needlessly severe with the girl. It was true that she seemed to be happy at the school and was making good progress. Her half-term report told him that. If he had sent her to the Chalet School only for the sake of her education, it would not have been so bad. But he had told her—and meant it—that it was a punishment for deliberate disobedience. He had never relented one iota. He had even spoiled her half-term holiday in his resentment. Even supposing she recovered from this accident, whatever it was, he felt that he must have forfeited her love. And she was his only child!

The journey seemed never-ending, but at last the stewardess came round, seeing that people had fastened their safety belts properly. A few more minutes and they were taxiing up the great runway. The plane stopped, the doors opened and the steps had been run up. He and Nanny were almost the first out, and as they reached the ground. a lady came hurrying up with hands outstretched. "Professor

146

Fry?" she asked. Then she turned to smile at Nanny. "And Nanny's come, too? Oh, good! Nanny, Richenda asked for you last night." She turned to the Professor. "I'm Miss Ferrars, Richenda's form mistress. I have the car here and it isn't too far to Berne."

"Berne?" he asked dully. "I thought the school was at the Görnetz Platz."

"So it is, but we were in Berne at the dentist's when it happened and Richenda was taken to the Eye Hospital. It's her eyes, Professor. A little brute of a boy squirted some ammoniac mixture straight into them. It was done in a moment—no one had any time to interfere. Matron and Herr von Francius had her at the Eye Hospital almost at once, though, and before that, he had filled the eyes with some oil to relieve the burning. The oculist said it was the best thing that could have been done and he hoped the sight might be saved at least. But she's in great pain. Here's the car. Will you get in at the back? Nanny, will you sit beside Miss Dene? She's our best driver at school, and thank goodness, there's no speed limit here! I'll come in at the back and you can ask me anything you want to know. O.K., Rosalie. Go ahead!"

Rosalie Dene let in her clutch and then they were bowling through the quiet streets. Kathie Ferrars pulled up a heavy rug round the Professor. When she had taken his hand, it felt icy cold. She blessed Matron for her forethought and fumbled in the basket at her feet for a flask of hot coffee. She poured out two cups, passing one to Nanny and almost forcing the other on the Professor.

"You must drink it, Professor. I know you've had a horrible shock, but we couldn't help it. Miss Dene tried to get you on the phone, but they said your phone was out of order at present, so we *had* to send the cable. Richenda's in no danger. But whatever that stuff was, it's hurt her eyes, and at the moment, they haven't been able to make a full examination to see exactly what the damage is. They've drugged her now and she's asleep and feels nothing, the doctor says. Miss Annersley is with her, of course. She came down the moment she could after I rang her and she's never left her since, except for when the oculist was with her. Please, drink up your coffee."

He drank it mechanically while Kathie went on chattering. She said later that she talked even on for the whole drive. Just how much he took in, she had no means of knowing. Much later, he told her that he thought her talk had saved his reason, and Kathie, who had gone on from sheer nervousness, could only be thankful that her tongue had been loosened.

Rosalie Dene made good her friend's boast that she was a fine driver. It was very little past the dawn when at length they entered Berne and in the great Augenklinik, all the lights were still on as they drew up outside the main entrance. Kathie jumped out and touched her companion on the arm. "Come along! We're here at last: Soon, you'll know all about it. Come along, Nanny!" She opened the other door and helped Nanny out. Rosalie followed, pausing only to lock the car. Then they proceeded into the building where Night Sister met them with professional cheeriness.

"So you've arrived safe!" she said in English with a strong German accent. "We are glad to see you, Herr Professor. Please, will you to come in here." She opened the door of a room and he stumbled in after her.

"May I see my daughter?" he asked, after a quick look round.

"But certainly—in von leetle minute. She is drugged, you understand. She knows nothing. But the pain in the eyes! And the shock to the nervous system!" Night Sister had a staccato manner of speech and it roused him from the apathy into which he had fallen.

"Is it—bad?" he asked.

Night Sister pursed her lips. "That we cannot say—as yet. Herr Fincke hopes to make a closer examination today. Then we shall know more."

"Will she—will the sight be seriously damaged?"

"As I said—we cannot say yet. Herr Fincke will come at nine and make examination, if she is aroused and the nerves rested. It may be that the—how do you say it?—the jet did not all enter the eyes, and they were only splashed. That is what we hope for. In that case, full sight will return, though it will mean wearing glasses. But that is nothing—nothing! If only we can save the sight! But now you may come," as a tap sounded at the door.

Nanny stood up at once. Night Sister looked at her worriedly. "I cannot let all to see her."

Rosalie spoke in her quick pretty German. "This is Nanny, for whom she has been asking, Sister."

"Ah! In that case, please to come. If she wakes she will be glad."

She led them out and along lofty, echoing corridors. By the lift, she turned, saying as they waited for it, "You will understand, Herr Professor. The eyes are closely bandaged. She cannot see you. But you may speak if she is awake and touch her."

They had given Richenda a private room, and she lay very straight and still in the narrow white bed. A shaded light burned in one corner and by it they could see that her eyes were heavily bandaged. Her face seemed to have shrunk and there were lines of severe pain about her mouth. She was very white; even her lips were pale. She moaned occasionally in her sleep and the Professor winced when he heard it. A young nurse had risen from the corner by the lamp and come forward, but Sister waved her back and herself explained to the Professor.

"She cannot feel any pain. These moans are quite—quite—involuntary? At least, they are without real meaning." She laid a hand on the wrist lying on the white sheet and kept it there a moment. "She is stronger now. The pulse is quieter. I think Herr Fincke will be able to make his examination today."

The Professor stood at the side of the bed, looking down at his girl. She looked such a child as she lay there. The rough red curls had all been brushed back to clear the bandages, and were scattered wildly over the pillow.

Nanny stumped forward and took the limp hand in hers. "My pretty! My baby!" she crooned. "Oh, my pretty girl! Nanny's here now!"

Richenda heard nothing. She still lay in that heavy,

drugged sleep which had mercifully put an end to her pain for the time being. Sister touched the Professor on the arm. "We must go now. She will sleep another hour and then Herr Fincke will come. You have had a journey. You must have Frühstück. See, Herr von Francius has taken a room for you in one of the hotels. I will give you the name downstairs. You will go there, and after a meal and perhaps a rest, you will come back. Then we may have news for you. Good news, I hope. But now, you can do nothing. Later, when all goes on well, she will be glad to have her papa with her. Come, now!"

Nanny looked across at her imploringly. "I'd like to stay, Madam. I could sit here and give her a drink or anything she wanted."

Sister shook her head. "Not now, but later," she added consolingly. "We will take good care of her. You shall come back soon. Now go with the Herr Professor and eat and rest."

Dearly would Nanny have liked to argue the point, but she recognised that she must not. She stumped out of the room after them, and Sister took them back to the little waiting-room where Miss Annersley had now joined her mistresses.

"We won't talk here, Professor," she said quietly. "Herr von Francius has rooms booked for you and Nanny at the Schweizerhof. Miss Dene will drive us there now, and you must have a meal while I tell you what I know."

It was something of a crush in the car, but they managed and it was not too far to the Schweizerhof where Rosalie decanted the Head and the other pair before driving off. She must get herself and Miss Ferrars back to school for the day's work and they would breakfast at Interlaken before tackling the mountain road up. And even driving at a pace that would have seen her in the police court for speeding at least half-a-dozen times, did not get them back at the Chalet School until most of the morning's church services were over. The girls arrived back twenty minutes later.

The Catholics were first to arrive, and the Maynard triplets made a beeline for the office to find out if Miss Dene had come back from Berne. She met them at the door and told them that there seemed to be a tiny improvement in Richenda. Then she added with a smile, "And your father has just been on the phone to me. Your mother has had her operation and has come through it splendidly. He has just seen her and she has roused up, had a drink of milk and fallen fast asleep. So you've nothing to worry about there. Please God, we shall be able to say that about Richenda presently. Now run along and take your things off and get ready for Mittagessen."

"Has Ricki's father come?" Len demanded.

"Yes, and her Nanny. I'm ringing up the hotel after Mittagessen and if you three obey me *at once*, I'll tell you what Miss Annersley says. Now be off!"

They fled on the word and were rewarded later by hearing that Richenda had roused out of her drugged sleep with less pain in her eyes, though Herr Fincke had thought it wise to put off the examination till a little later.

Miss Annersley was staying down until the examination was over. She went to the hospital with the Professor and Nanny in the afternoon, and waited for them with Matron who gave her rather more detail than she had done before.

"The right eye is decidedly better," she said. "Herr Fincke is almost sure that the sight will be completely restored to it. About the left, he is more doubtful. She has a good deal of pain there."

Upstairs, Richenda, lying with bandaged eyes, was nearly stunned to hear her father's voice shaking as he said, "My poor little girl! But they tell me they hope to relieve the pain entirely before long."

"Is—is it you, Father?" she asked weakly.

He laid his hand on hers and suddenly she was clinging to it. "Father! You'll tell me the truth, I know! You are very hard, but you never lie! Am I—am I—blind—for ever?"

"No," he said quietly. "Your eyes are bandaged now to give them a chance. But the oculist assures me that your right eye will probably be normal. The pain is nearly gone there isn't it? It may mean wearing glasses for a time, but you won't be blind. You—you must be thinking what sort of frames you would like and what colour," he added, startingly.

Richenda laughed feebly. "I don't really care so long as I can see again some time. And the pain isn't too bad now. It was awful at first."

"Yes, but that's over. If you go on improving as you are doing, Herr Fincke, your oculist, will make a thorough examination tomorrow. He even thinks the eyes may both come right in time. But it must depend on you, partly. You must try to keep quiet so that you get strong quickly. And Richenda! When Christmas comes, you shall have the Khang-he vase for your own. Now Nurse is making faces at me, so I suppose I must go, but I'll be back again soon. Nanny is coming to see you after tea and then no more visitors till tomorrow, I suppose. Good-bye, child. Keep up your heart. You'll be better soon." He bent and kissed her and then went away, leaving her nearly gasping with surprise.

Herr Fincke made his examination next day.

Her father was waiting for the verdict, unable to sit still, so anxious was he. At long last, the great man came, and his face as he entered told them before he spoke that it was good news.

Striding across the floor with broad smiles on his typically German face, he caught the Professor's hands in his and shook them vigorously. "Herr Professor, I give you joy! Das Mädchen will regain her sight. The right eye is but little harmed and the left will recover. Oh, not soon. There is great need for patience. But by the time she is twenty or twenty-one, she will cast aside her spectacles and see as well as ever."

Professor Fry released his hands as gently as he could.

"I am very thankful to hear you say it," he said. "I feel we owe a great deal to you and to the nurses and sisters of this fine place."

But if Professor Fry seemed to take it calmly, Nanny did not. She burst into tears and wept heartily. Miss Annersley felt choky, but she had her emotions under better control than Nanny. She held out her hand to Herr Fincke with a

152

few well-chosen words of gratitude and relief. At last, they got away from the excitable oculist, and were allowed to go and see Richenda. The bandage over the right eye had been removed, but the left one was still there. She beamed at them with the one bloodshot optic.

"It's all right, Richenda," her father said in his quiet voice. "You *won't* be blind. We may be very thankful. I know I am."

"Oh, so am I!" his daughter cried. "It's lovely to be able to see again, even if it's only with one eye and in such a dim light. But I shouldn't like it any brighter at present. Light hurts it."

"That will soon pass," Miss Annersley said with a smile. "And now I really must say good-bye to you for the next few days. The school needs me. I may be able to come down again later on in the week. But you won't need me. You have your father and Nanny now."

"Yes," Richenda agreed. "But I'd still like to see you some time, Miss Annersley. Herr Fincke says I must stay here for another fortnight for treatment, though he hopes that by that time, the eye will be much better and I can come back to school." Then she added anxiously, "Must I be out of the play?"

The Head laughed outright. "You don't sound as if you would need much longer here. No, you shall keep your part. Now I *must* go. Good-bye dear. Hurry up and get well. We shall all be glad to see you back again."

She went to be whirled back to the school, where she found waiting for her a long letter from Lady Russell, once Madge Bettany, and founder of the school. It told her that Joey, having come through the operation as well as anyone could wish, was now recovering by leaps and bounds and insisting that the middle of next week would see her and Jack off on their second honeymoon.

Chapter XVII

ALL'S WELL

RICHENDA did not take her part in the Christmas play after all. In fact, she did not return to school until the last week of term. The shock and pain she had endured had upset her nerves. She was thin and pale and jumpy, and the doctors advised the Professor to take her further south where it was hoped the warm soft air would steady her. So as soon as the left eye seemed to be healing, they packed up and went off to a little village in Ticino where they had rooms in a chalet, and the warmth, quiet, and as much rich milk as she could drink, soon mended the jangled nerves. Even so, there was no question of her return to school until after Christmas. However, she begged to go back for the play and her father agreed.

A letter from her to Freudesheim brought an instant invitation to all three of them to stay there for the few days of their visit, so it was with Mrs. Maynard, looking as if nothing had ever been wrong with her, that Richenda drove to St. Luke's Hall, the hall built close to the Sanatorium gates, all agog about the play.

Most of the girls were behind the scenes in the dressing-rooms, but Len, who was a herald, had dressed early, flung a great shawl over her fineries and was in the little portico, looking out for them.

"Your legs!" Joey said as she surveyed her daughter.

"What's wrong with them?" Len protested. "*I* can't help it if they're on the long side. Look at the height of you and Papa!"

"Oh, I know. But just now, you look *all* legs! Hurry up and talk, you two. It's chilly in this place and we're blocking up the entrance anyhow."

Len grinned and turned to Richenda with an eager question about her eyes.

"Oh, getting better, thank goodness!" Richenda replied. "The right one is nearly well again. The left isn't too good yet, but it will be in time. They all say so. How d'you like my glasses?"

154

"Len Maynard! What are you doing here?" exclaimed a well-known voice as Nancy Wilmot appeared. "Joey, I'm surprised at you encouraging her! Back you go! Hello, Ricki! Eyes better? Good! We're looking forward to having you back next term, so mind you don't disappoint us. Jo, your seats are in row D with the twins in front of you so that you can restrain them if they start anything. I must fly! It's nearly time for the overture!" And she turned and vanished, leaving Jo and Richenda to go in, each holding a twin's hand firmly, and take their places.

They got the twins safely into their seats and took their own, and just as Joey opened her programme, Mr. Denny, brother of Miss Denny and choir-master to the school, appeared on the conductor's rostrum and was welcomed by a round of applause. He bowed gravely and then turned to his orchestra, made up largely of pupils from St. Mildred's. He tapped on his desk and all instruments came to the "Ready". Then the glockenspiel played by the art master, Herr Laubach, rang out its bells in a Christmas peal, and the strings and woodwind swept into the overture.

As it ended, the curtains swept back to show a magnificent banqueting hall of the Middle Ages. A long table stood across the back of the stage with gaily-clad people sitting round it. In the centre were obviously the lord and lady— Hilary Bennet and Vi Lucy, two of the prefects—and a jester clad in blue and yellow was running round, hitting people with his bauble, cracking jokes—many of them so highly topical that the actors laughed most naturally. Suddenly, there came a thundering knock at the door and the herald appeared, gorgeous in quartered tabard, her long legs flashing redly as she strode to the centre of the stage, blew a blast on her trumpet—Joey put up her hands to her ears—and then said in stentorian tones, "A messenger from the king's grace! He has been benighted and desires to pass his Christmas here with you, my lord. He will be here anon!"

Instantly, all was bustle and excitement. A number of servants rushed in to straighten the table. A butler whisked off some of the empty dishes and everyone began to tidy their attire. This king was young and just recently crowned, and much was expected from him. He had great positions in his gift and more than one of the revellers speculated aloud as to what this might lead to.

Rosamund Lilley, one of the ladies, nearly convulsed Joey by remarking as she put her high horned coif straight, "He isn't *married* yet, you know. There's a chance for one of us. Do I look meet to be presented?" To which her opposite number, Gwen Parry from VIb, replied in unnaturally squeaky tones, "As meet as you ever do. But do you think a crown would go well with your nose, my dear?"

They had just got everything into order when the herald appeared again. But it was not the king he came to announce, but a couple of beggars who sought shelter for the night. The lord frowned, but the lady pleaded that it was Christmas night. The herald clinched it by saying, "They have a babe with them, lady." So the lord relented and the pair were brought in.

Tall Prunella Davies made an excellent man in a ragged brown tunic, baggy knickers to match, and a rough cloak flung over all. Barbara Chester of the fair curls looked very sweet as the woman in her shawl which she threw aside to reveal a real live baby. Mrs. Graves had been coaxed to let her younger daughter Loïs be carried on. Loïs was a very placid baby and she sat up in Barbara's arms and cooed at the audience.

Hilary Graves, seated at the end of the front row, ready to fly to the rescue if Loïs should start to yell, heaved a sigh of relief and sat back to hush Marjorie, her elder girl, who had bounced up to announce at the top of her voice, "Vat's my sister!" before anyone could stop her.

The ragged pair thanked the lord and the lady and humbly took a seat behind the table in accordance with the orders of the haughty butler, who bade them keep out of sight as the king himself was coming.

Another fanfare on the trumpet and the herald announced his lord's greatest enemy who had been lost in the snow-storm raging outside. The lord stood aghast, but once more the lady pleaded the night, and so he, too, was made welcome. At long last the king came, and Mary-Lou, truly regal in her crimson robes, with a circlet set on her sunny curls, strode in. He replied to the greeting of the company and then looked round.

"Heeded ye my forerunners?" he asked. "The beggar pair; the lost enemy? Are they here and welcome?"

The beggars came forward and Loïs created a sensation by leaning out of her stage mother's arms and holding out her hands to Mary-Lou. This was an unrehearsed effect, but Mary-Lou rose to the occasion. Stepping forward, she took Loïs who crooned and chuckled to herself as she grabbed at the gold paper chain the king wore round his neck. With superb self-possession, Mary-Lou gently held the small hands as she continued with her speech, the gist of which was that those who showed compassion on poor as well as rich, enemies as well as friends, were those he needed round him at his court. The lord was bidden prepare to attend as king's adviser and the lady was to take the place of royal almoner. The curtain fell on this and at once was raised to show a back-drop of a garden with a bevy of angels—the school choir—who sang very sweetly the old carol, *Quem Pastores*. As they finished, the curtains fell again, rising a minute or so later to show a Tudor scene, with children running in, the boys swinging skates, and the girls dancing gaily. They had been out to bring in the yule log and amid cheering, Joan Baker and Sue Meadows came in, dragging a log wreathed in holly, with the two smallest Juniors sitting astride it, waving their hands and cheering as lustily as the others. A lady in Tudor dress entered, and greeted them all, bidding them hasten for the Mummers would soon be there. Immediately the log was hauled to the enormous hearth behind the table and among them, they got it lifted on. And now came a grand effect. They had fixed coloured electric bulbs among the red and white papers and sticks that filled the hearth. Miss Derwent behind the scenes was waiting, and when the log was in position, she switched them on so that crimson and amber lights flared up inside the hearth, giving a very realistic effect of the log catching afire.

A bang at the door heralded the Mummers who marched in, singing the Mummers' carol. A brief Mumming play followed and the curtains fell as serving men and maids came in, bearing the traditional Christmas dishes of frumenty, plum porridge and grandest of all, the boar's head from which real steam issued, as a bowl of boiling water had been set inside the papier-maché model. From behind the curtains, came the voices of the choir singing the *Boar's Head Carol* and then there came the interval.

When the curtains opened again, it was to show the angel choir standing in serried rows, long scrolls held among them, and singing with all their hearts, *In the Fields with their Flocks Abiding*.

As the carol ended, the curtains fell and the choir sang again, this time, hidden, *Love came down at Christmas* to a tune composed by Mr. Denny himself. Then they rose to show the crown of the Christmas story—the stable at Bethlehem.

Verity Carey was the Madonna, very sweet and serious in her blue robes, bending over the trough in which lay the bambino they kept for this purpose. Behind her, stood Lesley Malcolm, the St. Joseph. A sheep, Joey's big St. Bernard, Bruno, and a tiny donkey stood at the foot of the trough. That was all that was to be seen in the softly-lighted picture. Then came the shepherds to kneel to worship at the manger. They were followed by the three kings, bearing the traditional gifts of gold, frankincense and myrrh. The people from the other parts of the play followed, all bringing offerings which the Madonna acknowledged by a slow raising of one hand. Finally, the angels trooped in and took their places in the shadowy back and sides of the stage. Tiers were there and soon the whole scene was lined with them, all in white to make a background for the gay colours of the mortals. The whole stage was flooded with amber light and the orchestra broke into the hymn with which all Chalet School nativity plays ended—the *Adeste*, sung in Latin.

"What a wonderful play!" Richenda said to Joey as, the curtains having fallen for the last time, she roused from the trance into which she had fallen. Joey, looking at her thought that, in spite of the glasses, she looked very well and she was certainly happy.

The school broke up on the Tuesday and the Frys stayed till then, for Richenda had to pack her belongings. He stayed at Freudesheim, but she, by dint of coaxing, got leave to spend that last weekend at school. They all came home early on the Tuesday morning to find Jack and the car waiting to take the Frys back to their temporary home in South Switzerland.

"Well," Joey said as she kissed Richenda good-bye, "how has it been, Ricki?"

Richenda knew what she meant. "It'll be all right now," she said joyfully. "Father really does understand and he says that when we go home, he'll begin to teach me about ceramics, a little at a time. He's quite different, Mrs. Maynard. I think someone must have been explaining things to him—Miss Annersley, perhaps. Anyhow, he does understand and I don't think we'll ever again try to make each other so miserable as we did before. I only wish I knew who it was that I could thank them. But I can't very well go barging in on the Head and ask her, can I?"

"Not if you want to remain alive!" Joey assured her with dancing eyes. Though Richenda was not to know it for a long time, her thanks had reached the right person, for Joey had made it her business to have a good talk with Professor Fry the very night she came home from her second honeymoon, and had seen to it that he did, indeed, understand.

"And you're glad you left Maggie's and came here?" she asked, knowing well what the reply would be.

"Glad? Well, what do *you* think?" Richenda retorted as she raced to the car where her father was calling to her to hurry up or they would miss their train. "I loved Maggie's when I was there, but the Chalet School really is *something*!"

Armadas are chosen by children all over the world. They're designed to fit your pocket, and your pocket money too – and they make terrific presents for friends. They're colourful, exciting, and there are hundreds of titles to choose from – thrilling mysteries, spooky ghost stories, hilarious joke books, brain-teasing quizzes and puzzles, fascinating hobby books, stories about ponies and schools – and many, many more. Armada has something for everyone.

Book Tokens

Give them
the pleasure of choosing
Book Tokens can be bought
and exchanged at most
bookshops

Armada